MURDER ON THE WICHITA

A Fen Maguire Mystery

MURDER ON THE WICHITA

A Fen Maguire Mystery

BRUCE HAMMACK

Chapter One

The hotel's smoke alarms blared, causing Fen to bolt upright in bed. Confused as to the date, time, and place, he swung his legs off the bed and dry-washed his face. It didn't take long to put things in order; he needed to get out.

"Bailey!" The single word escaped his lips as he reached for his boots beside the bed. Was she in her room? No—she'd slept a good portion of the way from Central Texas to Wichita Falls and wanted to burn off energy in the hotel's pool while he took an early-evening nap.

The alarms continued to shriek their warnings to get out of the building. He'd have to trust that Bailey found her way to safety. Wallet, keys, and phone from the nightstand went into the pocket of a Carhart winter coat. The brown, felt Stetson was the last item he grabbed.

In the hall, he joined several guests as they made their way to the nearest exit. He believed Bailey was downstairs in the indoor pool, but he banged on her door, anyway.

No answer, and the alarms continued their insistent screams. He smelled smoke, but it was faint and none oozed from the edges of the doors he passed. No time to play fire-fighter. He made for the end of the hall, held the door open for a family of five, and followed them into the stairwell. One flight down and through a door was all it took before he joined others in the rain and sleet.

Realizing he was at the rear of the building, he set out to circle around to the front, hoping to find Bailey. He also remembered that's where he'd parked his truck.

The first firetruck approached with sirens screaming and lights ablaze. It turned into the hotel's entry as he rounded the building's corner. A fire department supervisor's SUV had arrived by the time he made it to his truck. The windows of his new one-ton dually with a camper shell had frozen over. Fen turned the key and waited until the battery warmed the glow plugs before starting the diesel engine. He turned the heat on before stepping back into the elements to look for Bailey.

Because she was short of stature, it took a while for him to pick her out of the crowd. He jogged to her, taking off his coat as he approached. All she had on was her bathing suit, flip-flops, and a short cover-up, which was already wet.

His coat all but swallowed her whole, which was a good thing. "Let's get in the truck."

Sleet stuck to her wet hair, and her teeth chattered like dice in a leather shaker. That didn't stop her from saying, "J.W.'s coming too."

"J.W.?"

Fen looked at the young man standing at Bailey's side wearing only a bathing suit, boots, and a towel draped over his head. A lock of wet, coal-black hair hung down his forehead. This was no time for introductions or questions as all three were shivering and frozen rain blew sideways.

They piled into the truck, with Fen in the driver's seat, J.W. in the passenger's seat, and Bailey in his lap. Fen didn't much care for the thought of his nineteen-year-old ward sitting on the lap of the handsome young man, but the back seat held a full load of canvases and art supplies. The large center console meant necessity won the skirmish over propriety.

The chattering of their teeth kept time with the clatter of the diesel engine. He pushed up the engine's RPMs to twenty-five hundred to shorten the time until heat would fill the truck. It seemed to take forever, but warm air mercifully blew through the vents.

In the meantime, an additional firetruck arrived along with several police vehicles. Red and blue lights reflected off every shiny surface.

Bailey finally spoke as a second wave of first responders entered the building. "Fen, this is J.W. Ellison. I met him when we were here in September."

The young man looked to be the same age as Bailey. "Pleased to meet you, J.W. I was wondering why Bailey insisted on coming back to Wichita Falls in December. The monthly *After Hours Artwalk Festival* ended in October."

"J.W. studies art at Midwestern State University."

"Pleased to meet you, Mr. Maguire. I'm a huge fan of your landscapes. I insisted Mother buy the one you did of the Guadalupe River. She gave it to me as a birthday present."

His words sounded like they came from the bottom of an empty rain barrel. He was a tall, lanky young man, perhaps with a dose of Native-American blood in him as evidenced by the sparse facial hair.

Fen continued to study the young man's face. "I remember the sale, and your mother. Tell her how much I appreciate it." He paused. "Didn't you have a booth at the September art fair?"

"Yes, sir. Several of us students pitched in and shared the

cost. We made enough to cover our expenses with a little left over."

The wail of additional sirens split the night. A bevy of police SUVs arrived, followed by an ambulance.

"Something's wrong," said Fen.

Bailey shifted. "Duh. There's a fire."

Fen shook his head. "It's something else. Too many police."

The defroster had done its job, and the truck's windshield wipers made occasional passes that allowed them to see clearly. Another ten minutes ticked away and two unmarked police vehicles arrived.

"Look," said Bailey. "They're allowing guests to go inside."

"Uh-huh," said Fen. "They're going in, but only a few at a time. Let's wait until they get those poor souls out of the weather."

Rain and sleet-soaked guests reentered the building until only a couple who were smoking cigarettes remained outside. "Our turn," said Bailey. "I can't wait to get a hot shower."

The front door parted with a whoosh as the trio approached. The cold air lifted the garland on the eight-foot Christmas tree in the lobby and settled into place again as the door closed behind them. Two uniformed police officers met them.

"Room number?" said the first.

"203," said Fen.

The man raised his head and gave a sideways look. "Go to the first room on your right." He pointed to a long hallway that led to the elevators.

Fen took a couple of steps forward which cleared the way for Bailey to speak. The officer asked for her room number after staring at her longer than necessary.

"Bailey Madison. Room 204."

Both officers came on point and traded conspiratorial nods. "First room on your right."

That left J.W. and some stragglers behind him. "Name and room number," demanded the officer.

"I'm here visiting the young lady. As you can see, we were in the pool."

"Follow your girlfriend to the first door on the right."

"What's this all about?" asked Bailey.

Instead of answering, the second policeman issued a warning. "Do as you're told. First door on your right."

Fen bristled at the curt reaction but held his words in check. Bailey wasn't so inclined. "No need to be rude. It's not illegal to ask questions."

"If you say one more word, you're going in cuffs."

"One more word." Bailey gave the officer a hard stare. "I'm cold, tired, and not in the mood for a couple of rude cops."

The officer reached behind his back and produced a pair of handcuffs. "Hands behind your back."

Fen stepped forward. "Is your body camera on?"

The officer turned his attention to Fen. "It's a good thing I carry two sets. You're being detained, too."

"What's the charge?"

"Suspicion."

"That's not a crime. You'll need to do better."

"It's enough in this town. Give me your ID."

"It's in my back pocket. I'm not going to reach for it because as soon as I do, you'll say I was reaching for a weapon."

The officer pointed. "Hands on the wall."

The first officer joined in. "That goes for you lovebirds, too."

"Or what?" said Bailey.

"Or you'll go to jail for obstruction." He gripped the yellow and black tazer on his utility belt.

"Don't even think about it," said Fen.

The door opened to the room they'd been instructed to go to, and the family he'd seen on the second floor came out. Wide eyes took in the spectacle.

A plainclothes policewoman trailed behind the family and asked, "What's going on, Charley?"

"They're refusing to comply. Rooms 203 and 204. I've detained them."

"That's a lie. This jerk won't answer a simple question." Bailey faced the officer. "You still haven't told us why you're treating us like we did something wrong." She shrugged her shoulders and Fen's coat fell to the floor. She then pulled up her cover-up, showing a lot of skin and not much of a bathing suit. After turning a circle, she glared at the officer. "I'm ready for a pat down, if that's how you get your jollies."

Fen had his hands against the wall, but continued to look over his shoulder as the second officer took his wallet from his back pocket. He announced, "This guy's name is James Fenimore Maguire."

Fen said, "Run a 29 on me and check with NCIC before you make bigger fools of yourself."

J.W. found his voice. "Sheriff Maguire, can I insist on calling my mother now, or do I need to wait?"

Fen saw the woman he thought to be a detective roll her eyes. "Put the cuffs away and give the man his wallet. The young man is J.W. Ellison, Jr. After you two apologize, show them into the room."

Bailey picked up the coat, put it on, and zipped it all the way. "Hope you two perverts enjoyed the free look."

Fen shot her a gaze that spoke without words that she'd made her point and to pull in her claws. She'd come a long way from her wayward upbringing in Houston, but every now and then the old attitude toward authority reared its ugly head.

With the wallet retrieved, and without an apology, the three made their way to the open door. The detective closed it behind them. "Sorry again for the rough treatment. I'm Detective Margaret Sibley." She swept a hand in the direction of a man who scowled at them. "This is Senior Detective Jay Grimes."

Detective Sibley wore jeans, a western-cut shirt, puffy vest, and boots that looked like they'd seen plenty of wear. She was a tad bow-legged, indicating she likely was no stranger to riding a horse. The handshake was firm, like she meant to convey she was comfortable with shaking hands with a former sheriff. Moving only hazel eyes, her gaze fixed upon the young man. "Hello, J.W. How's your momma?"

"Busy as usual. She's in charge of the Christmas parade again this year." J.W. tilted his head. "What's going on? Was there a fire?"

The two detectives traded glances before the older of the two spoke, "We'll get to details in a minute, let me make sure we're clear on who everyone is. We know J.W. and his mother. In fact, everyone in a hundred miles knows her." He looked at Fen. "Did I hear you're Sheriff Maguire?"

"Former sheriff. I was a state trooper for ten years then sheriff of Newton County for another ten."

Detective Grimes snapped his fingers. "Maguire. Yeah, didn't you have to take a medical retirement from the highway patrol after someone shot you?"

Fen nodded. "I limped on that gimpy leg for years. I finally had a knee replacement."

A chill shook J.W., but he picked up the conversation. "Mr. Maguire is a world-class artist. He's taking over for Professor Shirley at MSU. The doctors have her on bedrest until the baby comes."

"I hear it's going to be a Christmas baby," said Detective Sibley.

Both detectives cast their gaze to Bailey. Fen answered their unasked question. "This is Bailey Madison. I guess you could say she's my protégé."

Bailey explained. "He's teaching me how to paint. I live in an apartment over his garage."

Fen and Bailey traded glances. "She's a promising young artist. Once I get the rough edges knocked off of her, she'll be ready to strike out on her own."

After trading nods, Detective Grimes got down to business. "Back to why we're here. The reason the two officers were so interested in you is because first responders found a body in room 205."

"That's next door to my room," said Bailey.

Detective Grimes nodded. "That was also the source of the smoke that set off the alarm."

"An overcooked bag of popcorn caught fire," said Detective Sibley.

Fen leaned forward. "A bag of popcorn doesn't explain the massive police response."

The senior detective seemed to choose his words with care. "We're treating this as a suspicious death."

There was much more to the story than what the detectives would say. Fen came to two quick conclusions: First, the three of them had nothing to do with the death of the person in room 205. Second, a ride to the police department's interview rooms might still be in their future.

Chapter Two

Detective Sibley stood. "We need formal statements from each of you. I'll go with you next door. There're plenty of tables and chairs so you can spread out."

Fen understood the reason for separating people while they wrote their statements. The detectives wanted accounts of events without cross-contamination. It's what he'd do if he were in their boots.

He looked at a harried couple with two young children and concluded their room must be near his and Bailey's. The mother tried her best to corral the youngest child while writing as fast as she could. The father had the eldest sitting on the floor beside him.

Fen sat at a desk that was far away from Bailey and J.W. Despite the detective's instructions, they chose to sit next to each other. Detective Sibley made her way over and handed him a boilerplate form with *Witness Statement* written across the top. Fen said, "I'm not sure I remember how to do this." He followed it up with a mischievous grin.

The woman played along. "I hear that all the time from exsheriffs staying in hotels where people die. Do the best you can."

"Ah," said Fen in a whisper. "I could tell by the overreaction of the two officers screening guests that this was a homicide. Is the victim a man I might know?"

She glanced around the room. "I doubt it, unless you subscribe to the local paper." She leaned over. "I'd love to tell you, but my partner would have me writing parking tickets. It's much too cold to be on foot downtown."

He held up both hands in surrender. "No problem. I wouldn't want you getting frostbite. Besides, the victim's name will be all over town within the hour."

"What makes you say that?"

"This city may have a population of over a hundred thousand, but it has a small-town feel. You didn't deny the victim was a male. The interest shown by you, Detective Grimes, and the two cops who wanted to arrest first and ask questions later tells me you know the dead man. More than likely, he's well known."

"Nice try, Sheriff Maguire, but I still won't give you the name." She tapped on the form. "You'd better get to work. Ms. Madison and J.W. don't look like they want to spend the rest of their evening waiting for you to complete your statement."

"Lucky for me, it'll be short. After a full day of driving, I was sound asleep until that rude fire alarm put an end to one of the best naps I've had in a long time."

She walked to the door and motioned with a crooked finger. One of the two officers they'd had the run-in with came in to proctor the room.

It took Fen five paragraphs to give the details of his reason for being in the hotel and his actions after the fire alarm sounded.

Detective Sibley waited for the three in the hallway. She looked at J.W. "Are your clothes in the pool area?"

"Uh... no." He looked like a little boy caught sneaking a Christmas cookie. "Actually, I left everything but my boots in Bailey's bathroom. That's where I changed."

Fen looked at Bailey with raised eyebrows. She came back with, "Where was he supposed to change? There's no dressing room by the pool."

"You can't go to your rooms until forensics finishes. Bailey's room adjoins the room where the man died." The policewoman shifted her gaze to Bailey. "Did you check the deadbolt on the door between the two rooms?"

"Why would I?" said Bailey with impatience. Her hair was wet and her feet had a purple hue to them. No doubt she was cold and miserable.

Bailey was on the verge of a major eruption. He'd challenged her morals and damaged their bond of trust. There was a perfectly logical explanation for J.W. being in her room and he'd assumed the worst. That hadn't set well with her.

He then realized Detective Sibley had done the same, but the question posed by the detective showed a probability Bailey and J.W. were suspects. He needed to act fast before Bailey's mouth earned them all a trip to a less comfortable place.

"Bailey," said Fen. "The three of us are going to the hotel's restaurant and have a nice, long dinner. I could use a cup of very hot coffee and a thick steak."

Bailey tried to tent her hands on her hips, but the sleeves of the coat hung below her fingertips. Frustration set in. "I look like a half-drowned cat, and my feet are blocks of ice."

The detective came to the rescue. "You won't be alone. Everyone on your wing of the second floor must wait in the restaurant or lobby until we go over their statements."

Fen tried to mollify her. "At least you're fully covered. My coat comes down to your knees."

The huff of air showed Bailey was unconvinced. "What about J.W.?"

Once again, Detective Sibley had an answer. "The hotel is providing blankets and fresh towels to anyone who stops at the front desk."

J.W. put an end to the conversation when he said, "Don't worry about me. I'll be fine as soon as I get a blanket." He turned to Fen. "I'll have to owe you for the meal until I get my wallet."

Fen shooed away the offer. "Your mother didn't quibble about the price of the painting. Consider us even."

Fen looked toward the front desk. "I'll get you both a blanket, and you can call your mom and let her know what's going on."

"She probably knows by now. Mom's network is amazing."

Bailey was on an even keel again. "I think your mom and our housekeeper have something in common. Thelma knows everything going on in the county, sometimes before it happens."

"That's Mom."

Fen didn't miss a beat. "I'd like to talk to her after you're finished. Let's find a quiet corner once I get those blankets."

"Get me a towel, too," said Bailey. She picked up locks of stringy hair. "At least I'll be able to wrap it up."

Fen strode to a table by the front desk. An unsmiling man wearing a maintenance worker's uniform stood beside stacks of towels and blankets. Stitched onto the man's navy-blue shirt was the name CARMINE.

"Two blankets and a towel, please," said Fen.

"Only one blanket and towel per guest." The man spoke

with an upper-Midwest accent he guessed to be Wisconsin or Michigan.

Using his finger as a pointer, Fen directed the keeper of the blankets and towels to Bailey and J.W. "They're for those two who were in the pool when the alarms went off."

"Oh. That's different."

"You're the first person I've ever met named Carmine."

"Plenty of Carmines in Chi-town."

Fen snapped his fingers. "I missed the accent. I thought it was Wisconsin or Michigan."

"You were close. My pa raised me in Madison, but I moved to Chicago after college."

"That's a long way from Wichita Falls, Texas."

"Tell me 'bout it."

Fen received the blankets, expressed his thanks to the worker and took steps to rejoin J.W. and Bailey. He wondered what string of events led a college-educated man from Chicago to work in a hotel in Wichita Falls, Texas. Everyone here had a story. He was glad the task of looking for a possible suspect among the guests and workers of a large hotel wasn't his job.

A random thought went through his mind. He hoped he wouldn't have to prove Bailey's innocence before this trip was over.

THE LOBBY WAS big enough that they found an alcove suitable for semi-privacy. Fen handed his phone to J.W., who punched in the number. It occurred to Fen that Hope Ellison's phone number was in his phone's memory now if he needed to call her again. Something told him he would.

The conversation between J.W. and his mother went without drama. The young man gave short answers to what seemed to be equally brief questions. He pictured an attorney asking questions in a deposition.

"She wants to talk to you."

He held out his hand to receive the phone. "You and Bailey grab a table and get something hot to drink. Coffee for me."

"Let's go," said Bailey. "My feet are like two frozen fish."

He waited until they'd taken several steps before putting the phone to his ear. "Hello, Mrs. Ellison. This is Fen Maguire. There's been a little excitement, but J.W. is fine."

"Let's cut to the chase, Mr. Maguire. Is it a homicide?"

Fen liked people who didn't waste time on niceties, but this was too direct. He decided he'd be just as direct. "It appears so."

"What makes you say that?"

"Twenty years of experience."

"Who's the victim?"

"The detectives wouldn't tell me, but I believe it's someone local."

"Why do you think that?"

"One detective said I wouldn't know who it was unless I subscribed to the local newspaper."

A long pause followed before Mrs. Ellison asked, "What are you doing for breakfast tomorrow morning?"

"No plans."

"Good. I'll meet you at the hotel restaurant at seven-thirty. Is there anything else I need to know?"

He put a hand behind his neck and massaged a stiff muscle. "I'm calling my attorney. There's a chance my protégé is going to jail tonight for more questioning."

"Does that include J.W.?"

"It's possible, even likely. Bailey's room has a connecting door to the room of the dead man. If I was still a sheriff, I'd be suspicious."

"Why?"

"J.W.'s clothes are there, as well as his wallet and keys."

"Expect a call from my attorney. Yours won't be able to keep J.W. from being interrogated tonight."

"Good idea. Call me back if you find out who the victim is."

"It won't take long."

She gave him the information about her attorney. He committed it to memory before the call disconnected without salutations.

He told his phone to call Chuck Forsythe. Chuck's wife, Candy, answered on the second ring. "How's the weather up north?"

"Lousy. If Chuck's available, you'd better put his phone on speaker."

"Chuck, it's Fen. He wants to talk to both of us."

Chuck's voice sounded next. "What kind of trouble are you in now?"

Instead of immediately answering the question, he said, "Candy, are you ready with paper and pen?"

"Whenever you go out of town, I keep something to write on in every room."

"There's a dead man in the room next to Bailey's. The rooms have a connecting door. The police may haul her in for questioning tonight. I'll give you the name and number of an attorney in Wichita Falls who'll represent her and a young man Bailey met in September who was with her tonight."

Chuck snickered. "Bailey's following in your footsteps. You both have a way of finding trouble."

"I beg to differ. It finds us."

Fen recounted what had transpired. He knew the information was incomplete, but it was enough for Chuck and Candy to get started.

Chuck summarized the account and said, "This doesn't

sound serious compared to your past exploits. I'm concerned about Bailey's mouth, though. Be sure to tell her not to say anything else without an attorney present. She's given them a written statement. That's plenty for one night."

"I'll tell both of them."

"Are you planning on investigating the homicide if it turns out to be one?"

"Not at this point. Unless I need to get Bailey out of hot water, there's no reason for me to look into it."

"Good. Thelma will skin all of us if you're not home for Christmas."

Candy asked, "Do you want me to call Lou and tell her?"

"Not yet. I'm having breakfast with the mother of the young man Bailey's interested in. She's a mover and shaker in this neck of the woods. I'll know a lot more tomorrow."

Chapter Three

Morning for Fen started the usual way. He made coffee in his hotel room and sat in a chair, speaking in hushed tones to the photo of his late wife, Sally. A grief counselor told him he'd eventually discontinue the practice, but he didn't see that happening anytime soon. He'd continue the habit until he couldn't feel her presence any longer. It hadn't waned through the years since her body rejected the heart transplant and she'd refused to get on the waiting list for another.

He told Sally about Bailey and J.W.'s very brief trip to the city police department after supper. Hope Ellison's attorney had derailed the detectives' attempts to question them. He told them the witness statements were sufficient for the time being, and he'd need to be present during any further questioning.

Bailey told him that Detective Grimes gave the attorney a stink-eye stare, but Margaret Sibley took it in stride, like she expected it to happen. Fen concluded it was old-school policing versus new.

After showering and shaving, he was ready to meet Hope

Ellison in the dining room. He saw her seated at a table, even though he entered the restaurant ten minutes early. He recognized her from their meeting in September when she purchased the birthday present for her son.

Dressed in ranch attire of jeans, boots, shirt, and vest she looked ready to wrangle cattle alongside her ranch hands. A light dusting of makeup and a thick sand-colored ponytail hanging down her back set her apart. He believed she could transform into a well-dressed, sophisticated woman whenever she put her mind to it, but breakfast with him didn't warrant the transformation.

"Good morning," said Fen. "I hope I didn't keep you waiting."

"I'm early. Did you sleep well?"

"Not very. What about you?"

"Tolerable. You know how it is running a ranch. There's always a sick horse or a cow that has trouble calving. Last night it was a son instead of a calf."

It surprised him that she showed no anxiety about the detainment of her son. Perhaps this wasn't J.W.'s first brush with the law, which is why she knew her attorney would handle things.

Fen wanted to ask how big her ranch was, but that would violate the unwritten rules of cowboy etiquette. Instead, he focused on the previous night's activity. "Did you find out the identity of the victim?"

Her response came with a quirk of her top lip. "His name is Charley Cleg, and there won't be many people grieving."

The server arrived and filled Fen's cup with black stimulant and asked, "Are you ready to order?"

"Not yet," said Hope in a no-nonsense tone. "Keep the coffee coming. It was a brief night."

Hope impressed him as a woman who was used to having

things her way. She was a decision-maker. He couldn't say he liked her dismissive way of speaking, but he appreciated her economy of words. He concluded she was a woman who spoke her mind and probably didn't realize how frosty she sounded.

"Tell me about Charley Cleg."

Hope pushed her coffee cup away so she could rest her hands on the table. "Charley made a name for himself as an investigative reporter for the local newspaper."

"I wouldn't think there was much need for that in a city this size."

Hope nodded. "There wasn't until he created the need. Wichita Falls was a stepping stone for him." She looked past him in a way that made him think she was recalling Charley's past exploits. "I should say, the people in Wichita County were his stepping stones. He kicked mud on a lot of decent reputations."

"Did that include yours?" asked Fen.

She nodded. "I need to back up and provide a brief history so you can get a better picture of the man. It all started with a property development scheme that went south and took many people down with it. A fast-talking, good-looking property developer by the name of Regina Cox sashayed into town about seven years ago. She set up shop as a real estate broker when the market was hot. She had a way about her that attracted men without offending women. Her smile could charm the horns off a steer. She could talk like a ranch hand or dress to the nines and fit in with the upper-crust women."

Fen nodded to keep her talking.

"After two years, she got her hands on a couple hundred acres, with five of them on the Wichita River. By then, she'd weaseled her way into the community and built a level of trust with everyone. She built a model home and put her plan in place. For the locals with money, she offered a stake in the development. For other locals, she sold them the best lots. She priced the lots on the low side of the appraised value and promised a beautiful riverfront home at an amazing price. She had a photographer take amazing photos of the model home."

Fen rested his chin on his palm. "What went wrong?"

"What we didn't know until it was too late was, that she'd advertised the riverfront property to out-of-state investors as well. She'd set up two investment companies; one for locals and another for out-of-state investors. It was a hit-and-run targeted sale. All certified checks for the full amount. Every sale took place on the same day. Financing for locals had to be arranged from one bank only."

He groaned as the magnitude of the scam became clear. "What prison is she in?"

"That's the problem. After taking in a massive haul of money in one day, she transferred the money and disappeared like dust in a rainstorm."

He leaned back and shook his head in unbelief. "That's one well-planned, executed crime. How much did she get away with?"

"The best estimate is seven million."

"How much did you lose?"

She didn't hesitate. "Three hundred thousand, but I was lucky. My CPA told me it helped offset the taxes on oil revenue."

He tilted his head and asked, "What does this scam have to do with the death of Charley Cleg?"

"Let's order, and I'll tell you."

Fen recognized this as another tactic Hope employed. It meant she controlled the pace of the conversation.

With orders placed, he sipped coffee until Hope was ready to answer his question. She looked around the room before bringing her gaze back to him. "I have to hand it to Charley

Cleg. He was one heck of an investigative reporter. He dug and dug until he had the names of every person in Wichita County who invested in Wichita River Estates. Over a six-month period, he wrote weekly columns giving the names of people snookered and how much they'd lost."

Fen puffed out his cheeks and let out a blow. "That means there's no shortage of people who will enjoy spitting on his grave. Who are the big losers?"

She took a drink of water. "There're two answers to that question. The first group was people who couldn't afford to invest. The second group is more interesting. They lost a lot more than money."

"I don't understand."

She held up her hand and lifted an index finger. "Mason Cleg. He's Charley's brother. A fair number of people believe he knew about the scam. Others simply hate him now because his last name is Cleg."

"Do you think he knew?"

Her head swung back and forth. "He lost money with the rest of us. Being his brother didn't stop Charley from putting Mason's name in bold print."

A second finger extended from a clenched fist. "Cleo Clayton was a big loser. She was vice president at the bank that handled most of the loans. She lost her career, her home, and her husband. What's left is a shell of the woman she used to be. I understand she's on strong anti-depressants. It's a shame about Cleo. The bank's board of directors threw her under the bus when they were the ones approving the loans."

Hope continued on, "A fair number of people blamed Hap Sibley for their losses. He was sheriff. Charley all but crucified him with criticism. Hap was a good sheriff, but after what Charley wrote, he didn't stand a chance in the next election."

"Sibley?" asked Fen. "Is he kin to Detective Margaret Sibley?"

"Her father."

Fen was on the verge of information overload, but Hope kept talking. "If you want to know who has something against Charley, get back issues of the paper and take your pick. There's also Charley's ex-wife, Lisa Stuart."

Fen hoped his eyes didn't show too much surprise. "Do you mean he mentioned his wife in one of his articles?"

"Ex-wife. It was all part of his plan to get out of Wichita Falls. Even though Lisa had already moved, she heard about the investment opportunity and lost money with the rest of us suckers. He ridiculed her without mercy. They'd separated long before Regina Cox slithered into town, so she was fair game along with everyone else."

It occurred to Fen what a high mountain Detectives Sibley and Grimes had to climb if they were to solve Charley's murder. No wonder they'd hoped to get a quick arrest of someone from out of town. He had to make sure Bailey didn't become a convenient scapegoat for an old-school detective on the downhill side of his career.

Hope interrupted his thoughts when she asked, "Where are you and Bailey staying while you teach at the university?"

It took a few extra ticks of the clock for Fen's mind to change gears. "Uh... Bailey's supposed to stay in a spare dorm room, and I'm to stay in an empty apartment on campus."

"Those apartments are dumps. Why don't you two come stay at the ranch? My late husband wanted six kids and built our home to give them each their own bedroom and bath. A kick in the head from a spirited horse cut short his plan of turning me into a broodmare."

Fen liked the idea of staying on a ranch, plus Hope was a walking computer for all things related to Wichita County and its occupants. Besides, he'd been looking for a location where he could paint a Northwest Texas landscape. What better place than a working ranch?

The only reservation he had was regarding Bailey. How would she feel about living under the same roof as J.W.?

Breakfast plates placed before them brought a pause to the conversation. Fen unrolled his napkin and promised to give Hope an answer that morning before the eleven o'clock checkout deadline.

Hope stabbed a bite of sausage. "I'll be in town all day in meetings concerning the Christmas parade."

"Are you in charge?"

She raised the meat laden fork halfway to her mouth. "I'm in charge every year."

Hope popped the bite in her mouth and chewed until she could speak. "I'll call my housekeeper and tell her to get two rooms ready." She raised her coffee cup to take a sip, then stopped. "I'm not pleased that J.W. changed clothes in Bailey's room yesterday. That's a recipe for trouble."

"Bailey has boundaries she doesn't cross."

"That's good to hear, but I believe in keeping my friends close so I can keep track of them."

Before he could pull the words back, Fen completed the saying. "...and your enemies closer?"

This earned a smile. "I like a home-field advantage."

Hope wasted no time leaving after she finished her meal. This left Fen a chance to think and review the events of the last twelve hours. His imagination strayed to all the victims. Greed had affected how many lives?

He had little doubt that Jay Grimes and Margaret Sibley had a Herculean task ahead of them in finding Charley's killer among so many suspects. He whispered, "Good thing I'm not involved in the case."

Chapter Four

en sat alone in the hotel restaurant talking into his phone. Even though he wasn't involved in an investigation, something inside told him to dictate notes while they were fresh on his mind. He didn't know what compelled him to do so; the murder of Charley Cleg was a matter for the police. Was it a habit born of twenty years in law enforcement? Perhaps it was the gnawing feeling in a deep place he couldn't readily identify.

Another thought came to him. Was it possible that Carmine, the maintenance man, had been a victim? There must be a story behind his move from Chicago to Texas. He shelved the thought for the time being. If he ran into Carmine again, he might ask.

After saying, "Lisa Stuart, ex-wife," he changed the phone's screen and called Bailey. She sounded more awake than he expected given last night's ordeal of being detained and taken to police headquarters. "How long have you been awake?"

"Long enough to brush my teeth."

"Come to the restaurant. I may have scored us a better place to stay."

"Where?"

"You'll find out when you get here."

The call cut off, which didn't surprise him. Even on a good day, Bailey wasn't a morning person. With the phone still in hand, he called Chuck Forsythe at his law office. Candy answered. "Good morning, Fen. How's Bailey?"

"Grumpy. I wanted to thank you and Chuck for getting in touch with that attorney."

Chuck's voice came over the speaker. "He's the best money can buy in Wichita Falls."

"I thought so. Bailey was in and out before her mouth got her in trouble."

"You won't have to worry about a repeat of her or J.W. Ellison being detained." Chuck cleared his throat and changed the tone of his voice. "By the way, there are some important people in that corner of the state who want you to look into something and it isn't the murder."

Fen let out a soft groan. Chuck and his band of justice seekers were the reason he now carried a private investigator's license. Except for Chuck, he didn't know who they were, but they always seemed to know where he was in the state. More than once he'd been asked to investigate a situation. Up to this point they'd all involved a murder. "How did I know you were going to say that? Let me guess. Does it have to do with a shady real estate broker who fleeced people out of millions and vanished without a trace?"

"It seems you've already sniffed it out. That's good. I'm sending Lou to help with research."

Fen sighed in resignation. "Have her call me when she's on the road."

"Anything else? My first client of the day is waiting."

"One more quick thing. Hope Ellison, J.W.'s mother, who seems to be the *grand dame* in Wichita County, wants Bailey and me to stay at her ranch while I'm teaching at the university. What do you think?"

Instead of Chuck responding, Candy's voice came to him. "Do it. I looked her up since our last conversation. Nothing of significance goes on in Wichita County that she doesn't know about. Her ranch is measured by the square mile instead of acres."

The sound of beeps from an incoming call came from Chuck's phone. "I need to go. Watch where you step on the ranch."

The abrupt end to the conversation left Fen staring at his phone and into his future with more questions than answers—the first being how to find Regina Cox. She'd vanished like someone touched her with a magic wand. Surely the former sheriff, Hap Sibley, had done an extensive search for her. How could her trail have gone ice cold so quickly? Was he somehow involved in the scheme and allowed her to fade away? Hope had described him as a good sheriff. How good could he be if he couldn't find a high-profile woman? After all, he had significant resources at his disposal.

His thoughts were interrupted when Bailey plopped into a chair opposite him. She looked the worse for wear after the night she'd experienced. She'd stuffed hair under a baseball cap and wore flannel pajamas.

"Nice PJs," he said in a mocking tone.

"I'm practicing."

"For what?"

"You told me I had to go to classes with you at MSU. I'm dressed the way college girls dress for early classes." She pushed her lips to one side. "Tell me again what MSU stands for."

"Midwestern State University. It's part of the Texas Tech University system. They offer a bachelor's degree in art."

He then told her about his phone call with Chuck and Candy and their new assignment. She sat up straighter as he spoke. "Are you sure I need to go to class with you? Lou might need help, and you have a habit of finding things for me to do when there's a murder to solve."

"No murder this time." He reconsidered the finality of his words. "At least not yet. Our assignment is to find a woman who stole millions of dollars."

"You're not telling me everything. I called J.W. on my way downstairs. He said you and his mother met for breakfast. What was that about?"

Fen sidestepped the question for now. He folded his hands on the table and spoke as if he couldn't decide something important. "J.W.'s mom suggested we stay at her ranch. I told her I'd need to talk to you first."

"What's to decide? I've stayed in a college dorm before. It pretty much sucks."

He knew his next words would light the fuse of a firecracker, but he said them anyway. "Do you think you and J.W. can behave yourselves?"

Her eyes narrowed. "If we were going to do anything, it would have happened yesterday when he changed in my room. For your information, you dirty-minded old man, I left him alone in my room to change while I went to the pool."

With palms raised, Fen said, "No need to snap my head off. You could have told me that last night." He moved on quickly. "Did you put that detail in your witness statement?"

"No." The single word snapped like she'd broken an icicle.

"What about J.W.? Did he?"

"Ask him."

Fen leaned forward and whispered, "Stop being offended for a minute and think. There's a connecting door in your room. Someone murdered the man in the room next to yours. J.W.

was alone in your room. It's possible he had access to that room."

"How? There's a door on both sides."

"Was the door on your side locked when you arrived in your room?"

"I don't know. Both sides would have to be unlocked for anyone to get into that room."

"Correct, but you don't know that they were or weren't."

Bailey wouldn't go down without a fight. "J.W. had no reason to go into the room next door. It's ridiculous to think he would."

Fen cut her off. "You've moved on to motive before we finished talking about means. There's at least one way to get into an adjoining hotel room without breaking down the door."

"How?"

"It's illegal, so don't get any ideas."

She shrugged. "So is hot-wiring a car. There's a big difference between knowing how and doing something." Curiosity overrode anger as she scooted forward in her seat. "Tell me."

Fen looked around to see if anyone was close enough to hear in order to pull Bailey into the story and away from her anger. "An extra-strong magnet. They don't use locks with keys for the doors to adjoining rooms, only dead bolts."

Revelation shone in Bailey's blue eyes. "I get it. You stand in your room with your pass-through door open. Put the extra-strong magnet against the adjacent door where the latch is and move the magnet. Click. You're in. How cool."

"Cool and illegal," said Fen as a reminder.

"Is that the only way it can be done?"

"No, but that's enough for one day. Let's get back to motive."

"Here we go again. You've already found a reason for J.W. to kill someone. I knew he was too good to be true."

Fen took in a deep breath and launched into the story of Regina Cox's real estate scam and Charley Cleg's reporting of the story. He gave special emphasis to Charley's characterization of the duped investors' ignorance. "According to Hope, not only were they easily deceived, but Charley implied duplicity and possible criminal involvement. She also said the reporter made thinly veiled accusations of collusion involving several prominent locals, which included the former sheriff, the vice president of a bank, and Hope Ellison."

He wanted to see if Bailey's emotions were still overriding her logic. "Do you see why those two detectives detained you last night? They knew it was a long shot, but J.W. had the motive, means, and opportunity to kill the man in the room next to yours. That reporter ran his mother's good name and reputation through a feedlot of rumors and innuendos. For some people, that's an excellent motive for murder."

Bailey pursed her lips as she seemed to process the wealth of information. After several seconds, her lips flattened into a straight line. "I still don't believe J.W. had anything to do with that creep being killed. By the way, how did he die?"

"Beats me. Hope probably knew this morning when we talked, but she didn't mention it. Doesn't matter at this point. We'll find out soon enough."

"Why doesn't it matter?"

"We're looking for a missing scam artist, not someone who killed a man with enemies all over the county."

Bailey cocked her head. "Is there any chance of a reward if we find Regina Cox?"

"Great question. Why don't you and Lou look into that?"

Bailey seemed to be back on level emotional ground. "You're going to like Hope Ellison's ranch and home. J.W. sent me photos when I told him we were coming back to Wichita Falls."

"I guess that's your way of saying we should take Hope's offer to give us a place to stay until classes end at the university."

"Or longer, if we're still looking for Regina Cox." She seemed to look longingly into the future. "Perhaps it will snow while we're at their ranch. I've never painted a winter scene of miles and miles of rolling plains."

Fen could almost see the cold desolation. "Come to think of it, neither have I."

The server arrived wearing a Rudolph pin with his red nose blinking. "It looks like you two are finished with your top-secret meeting. Are you ready for breakfast, sugar?"

Bailey didn't hesitate. "The three-egg omelet with biscuits and gravy."

It was a marvel of nature that Bailey could pack away food the way she did while maintaining such a slim figure. He wondered if she was still making up for the meager rations she received as a wayward child in Houston.

When her breakfast arrived, Bailey dove in like she hadn't eaten in two days. She sopped her last bite of biscuit in gravy and looked at him with inquisitive eyes. "What's the plan for the day?"

Fen glanced at the clock on his phone that lay on the table. "I'll call Hope and ask her when she wants us to arrive."

"That's so old school. Let me handle this." She retrieved her phone from a pocket in her pajama bottoms. Two thumbs attacked the keyboard. A reply came before he could take a good drink of coffee.

"J.W. said we can come any time. It's too muddy to do much of anything but paint this morning. He'll let his mom know."

Fen took out his phone and stabbed one letter at a time with his index finger until he'd finished his message to Lou.

Bailey rolled her eyes. "There's a faster way to do that."

"I know. It's making a phone call."

A huff signaled Bailey found him hopeless. She regrouped and said, "Now that I'm not staying in the dorm and Lou and I have things to work on, do I have to listen to you lecture classes?"

Fen pushed his coffee cup away from him. "You've already heard my pearls of wisdom. I'd rather see you painting, helping Lou, and being available. Find out what you can from J.W. about Regina Cox. His perspective on the fraud might be helpful."

"That's the best assignment you've ever given me."

Fen tilted his head down like he was looking over the tops of invisible eyeglasses. "Don't enjoy the assignment too much."

Bailey's parting mischievous smile bothered him more than if she'd argued or accused him of trying to run her life. She was a mature young woman, but there remained a lot of vulnerable little girl in her.

Calling Lou rose to the top of his to-do list, but Detective Sibley's arrival in the hotel restaurant rearranged his priorities. Worry lines etched grooves in her forehead as she took Bailey's recently vacated seat. "This won't take long. I came to warn you. A certain detective I know is hoping you'll start investigating Charley's murder so he can arrest you for interfering."

"Let's talk about that."

Chapter Five

The server brought a carafe of coffee without being asked. She filled Detective Sibley's cup and said, "Good morning, Margaret. It's been a while."

"Hello, Sadie. How's Matt and little Matt?"

"Big Matt's hot-to-trot about hunting. Little Matt's not so little. Still young enough to sit on Santa's lap, but this may be the last year."

While the two chatted, Fen made note of the detective's appearance. Keen eyes seemed to take in all that was happening in the room. She wore brown wool slacks with flared legs that fit over rust-colored boots. A tweed jacket with patches over the elbows covered a taupe blouse. It was a business-casual look that conveyed relaxed professionalism. Fen thought of his late wife Sally. She'd dressed much the same as she went off to teach school. He enjoyed the memory while the two women gabbed about the upcoming Christmas parade.

Margaret declined the offer of breakfast. She waited until the server couldn't hear their conversation. "Like I was saying,

Detective Grimes is none too happy about how things turned out last night."

"I can't say that I blame him. He knows Hope Ellison pulled some strings."

The detective lowered her voice, "The chief yanked Grimes's choke collar like he was a barking Doberman. It's a good thing Bailey was with J.W. Without Hope Ellison, that young lady would still be in jail."

Fen didn't doubt Hope had that kind of clout, but the detectives didn't know about his relationship with Chuck Forsythe. The level of Chuck and Candy's influence around the state still amazed him. The husband-and-wife team was an enigma. On the surface they appeared to be a country lawyer and his office-manager wife. Yet, when either of them made phone calls, influential people across the state paid attention and things happened.

Since there was no need to mention Chuck and Candy at this stage of the investigation, he changed the subject. "Do you think you would've gone into law enforcement if your father wasn't the sheriff when you were growing up?"

She gave him a curious look. "Did you hear me say Detective Grimes is gunning for you?"

"I understand," said Fen. "I'll take care of it before Monday morning when I go to the university. He'll find out there's no reason to worry about me when he learns we're leaving the murder investigation to the two of you. I'm looking for Regina Cox."

Margaret ran her tongue over her top front teeth before she challenged him. "To begin with, you may be a good private investigator, but my father used every resource at his disposal to find Regina Cox. I took up the search after he lost his bid for reelection. He made copies of all his notes. He and I still follow up on leads in our spare time."

"Perhaps fresh eyes might help?" He phrased it as a question to see how she'd respond.

"Not likely. Daddy was a smart, determined lawman. He used profilers, criminologists, and Texas Rangers. I even paid a medium to give me answers." She puffed out her cheeks and shook her head in disgust. "That was a waste of five hundred bucks."

"Did you tell your father about the soothsayer?"

Her eyelids parted wide. "Are you kidding? He would have taken me behind the barn and used a leather belt as a reminder not to be stupid." She spoke with absolute certainty. "Regina Cox didn't exist before she appeared in Wichita Falls."

Fen wasn't having any of it, but he didn't want to alienate a potential gold mine of accumulated information. This would be like walking a tightrope. He'd need to stroke Margaret before he poked her, so he changed the subject. "You're a smart detective. Is there a link between Cleg's murder and the disappearance of Regina?"

She scratched her neck under her right ear. "I lost most all of last night's sleep thinking about that very thing. The only link is they both made money from other people's misery. Regina stole money and trust. Charley stole reputations and landed a higher-paying job. Otherwise, they lived in two different worlds."

"That's the only link I see, too," said Fen in a weak voice. "It seems you and your father have exhausted every resource to find Regina." He let the thought hang in the air before saying, "Except one."

Margaret cast him a skeptical stare. "We tried everything."

"Almost," said Fen. "Did you ever consider asking a top investigative reporter to help you look for her? It sort of follows the adage that it takes one to know one. In this case, it may take a pushy reporter to find things you might have missed."

Frustration filled her response. "We didn't need to ask another reporter. Charley did his own investigating and wasn't shy about claiming unconfirmed sightings of Regina in various states. He concluded the series with a story stating she was living the high life in a country without an extradition treaty. He refused to give Daddy his sources, so he couldn't confirm or deny the validity of Charley's claims."

Fen stated the obvious. "And now Charley is dead and your last link to Regina Cox is gone." He leaned forward. "Are you going to give up looking for her?"

Margaret spoke through clenched teeth. "Never."

"I'm glad to hear it. One of the top investigative reporters in the state is on her way to Wichita Falls today. Her name is Lou Cooper. She works with me and Bailey, usually on murder cases."

A flash of hope came to Margaret's eyes and dimmed just as fast. "Grimes hates journalists, and he's the lead detective. Even if I wanted to help you, he'd block anything I suggested."

Fen looked beyond Margaret at nothing in particular. His words flowed out in a whisper, "There're two crimes: Fraud and murder. We need to get you assigned to finding Regina and leave Grimes to pursue the murder investigation."

"Good luck with that."

"It won't be luck."

"You have enough pull to do that?"

"Not me, and it's best if you don't know anything more about this." He paused and brought his gaze fully upon her. "For this to work, you'll need to allow me and Lou access to the file your father compiled."

"I live with Daddy on our ranch east of town. Everything related to Regina Cox is under lock and key. He won't allow it to leave the property."

"We can work around that."

A fly in the ointment occurred to him. "Lou's a plain-spoken woman. I'm guessing your father is, too. They might butt heads."

"Count on it. Daddy's opinion of journalists isn't much better than Detective Grimes's."

Fen couldn't help but smile. "This may be a Christmas to remember."

Margaret clasped her hands together in what looked like a prayer. "I appreciate your optimism in finding Regina, but I'm having a hard time believing you and a reporter will succeed where so many others failed."

Fen agreed but decided to put a brighter spin on it. "You said it would be me and Lou alone. Get used to the idea of adding your father and yourself to the team." He let his words sink in a moment. "Let's take it a step at a time. The first thing is to separate you from Detective Grimes. Tell me if I'm wrong, but I sensed he'd prefer to work with a different partner."

"He's resented me from day one." She flipped her hand like she was clearing away a foul smell. "He believes they promoted me because I'm the daughter of Hap Sibley. It's true I was the youngest applicant, but I was the only one with a master's degree in criminal justice. I also made it a point to work over-time when asked and volunteered to cover shifts on holidays. It seemed the thing to do since I'm single."

"That's impressive," said Fen. "I'm glad to see they rewarded merit and initiative. It must be tough working with Grimes."

She shrugged off the comment. "He's not so bad, just tired and ready to retire. So many changes have taken place since he was a rookie. He remembers the way things used to be and wants to turn back the calendar."

"I'm about the same age as Grimes, but I've moved on. Some people have a tendency to put on rose-colored glasses when looking back. I have to remind myself of the way things really were that long ago. They weren't so great."

The philosophical discussion ended, and Margaret stood. "Until you hear otherwise, watch out for Detective Grimes. He can be a nasty piece of work if he puts his mind to it."

Fen waited until the morning's latest tablemate cleared the room before taking his phone in hand. "Hope Ellison," he said into the device. When the call went to voice mail, he remembered the Christmas parade meeting she was chairing. The voicemail prompt ended with a beep. "Hope, it's Fen. Call me when you can. I need to cash in a favor I haven't earned yet."

If nothing else, the message would intrigue her enough that she'd respond quickly. His next call went to Lou.

Chapter Six

"Are you on the road yet?"

It was a throwaway question. The road noise coming from Lou's phone told him she was.

"I learned a long time ago to keep a go-bag packed. I'd be farther along, but Thelma made me stop by your place and pick up Christmas cookies for you and Bailey. She pumped me for information, but there wasn't much I could tell her. I'm glad you didn't fill me in before. She's better than the CIA with interrogations."

Fen relayed what he knew so far. It took the better part of twenty minutes.

Lou summarized the briefing. "I'm driving halfway across the state to find a woman who's been missing for years after she stole millions of dollars."

"Correct."

"And we're not working on a murder case that happened yesterday in the hotel I'll be staying in?"

"That's right."

"And Bailey is a suspect in the murder case."

"She did nothing wrong other than make a few cops mad at her. Our focus is on the missing woman and the money."

"What aren't you telling me?"

The question was classic Lou Cooper. She assumed there was always another layer, so she kept digging.

"You probably know the victim of the murder. It's a journalist named Charley Cleg."

"I know him by reputation. He's a scumbag."

Fen corrected her. "Past tense. He was a scumbag. There's a chance the two investigations will overlap, but we need to tread lightly. The lead investigator in the murder case is an old-school detective who hates journalists."

"I'm used to that from cops."

A horn honked, and Lou let the driver know she didn't appreciate the interruption to her conversation.

"Where are you?"

"Lampasas. Taking the back roads. That old coot honking didn't appreciate me not moving when the light turned green." She paused. "What were we talking about?"

"Being careful and remembering we're not to interfere in the murder investigation."

"Even though it could be linked to the missing woman?"

"Maybe it's linked, maybe it isn't. Either way, we're headed for trouble if we butt in."

Lou countered with, "That's what makes our assignments so challenging and rewarding."

He ignored her challenge, and added another nugget of information before he signed off. "By the way, Bailey and I won't be here when you check in. We scored rooms at a ranch owned by the mother of the boy Bailey's interested in."

"Good Lord," said Lou. "I'm clutching my pearls and going to the fainting couch. If Thelma catches wind that Bailey's staying with a love-starved cowboy, she'll come with a loaded shotgun. It'll be a toss-up to see if she wants to shoot you or the cow-pasture Romeo first."

Fen had heard enough. "Drive safe, Lou. Call when you get settled in. There's plenty of research for you. You'll need to scour old issues of the local newspaper. I'm close to getting access to the former sheriff's file on the fraud case, but that's not a done deal yet. For now, Regina Cox is your target. Find out everything you can about her."

"I remember reading about the case. Didn't surprise me."

"What does that mean?"

"Search *'the world's smallest skyscraper.'* This isn't the first case of fraud in that city."

A call waiting notification sounded in Fen's ear. "Got to go. Another call is coming in. Drive safe. Call when you get settled."

Fen ended one call and answered the next.

"Talk fast, Fen," said Hope. "The two biggest banks in town are locking horns about who'll be first in the parade. I told them to take five minutes and work it out between themselves before I moved them both to the end of the line."

Fen used as few words as possible to explain that he needed Margaret Sibley away from Detective Grimes to help him find Regina Cox.

"Consider it done. If there's the slightest chance of recovering some of the money stolen by that witch, I'll make sure you get all the help you need. I'll also call Hap and encourage him to help you. He's a prickly old cuss, but he'll do anything to make Regina pay for all the hurt she caused."

"Does that include working with a female reporter?"

"She'll need a thick skin, and you'll need to pave the way. Being a former sheriff will give you an edge, but fur's likely to fly when you throw a female reporter at him." She chuckled. "I'd like to see them square off."

"Lou can hold her own with the best of them."

"Got to go. Raised voices tell me those two old goats aren't willing to budge."

She changed the subject. "J.W.'s at the ranch waiting for you. I've another meeting this morning and a lunch appointment with the mayor. Make yourself at home."

The call came to an abrupt end. Fen leaned back and congratulated himself on the progress he'd made. He was well on the way to getting a talented young detective added to his team. That would give him access to law enforcement resources and a former sheriff's file on Regina. It was like finding a treasure trove, and would also allow him to put distance between himself and a grudge-holding senior detective.

The icing on the cake was that he and Bailey would have access to a ranch with vistas to paint, or at least sketch. The actual painting could take place in their studios at home. It was a good morning's work.

His mental pats on the back ended as he noticed Bailey standing in front of him with her head shaking side to side, hands on hips. "Why are you still sitting here acting like you're on vacation? Get off your duff and pack. J.W.'s waiting on us."

She turned and walked away before he could respond. So much for self-congratulations.

It didn't take him long to pack and meet Bailey in the lobby. She greeted him with a sneeze.

"You're not getting sick, are you?"

"Don't say that! You'll jinx me."

Fen gave her a sideways glance. "You know what'll happen if Thelma finds out you have so much as a sniffle?"

She answered with a piercing gaze. "I absolutely refuse to get sick."

Fen hoped she was right, but another sneeze didn't bode well. "Stay here. I'll get the truck."

The trip to Hope's ranch passed with Fen doing almost all the talking. He turned off the farm-to-market road onto a paved road leading to a massive home about a quarter mile to the west.

"Stop the truck!"

They'd made it only a hundred yards down the road when he glanced at Bailey and knew what would come next. Tires dug into the asphalt. Her door flew open before he came to a complete stop. The seat belt kept her from falling out as she retched.

He located a stack of restaurant napkins in the center console and handed them to her, along with her half-full bottle of water from the center cup holder.

When the dry heaves ended, she wiped her face, blew her nose, and rinsed her mouth. A mournful groan preceded her closing the door with a weak click. Her mottled face signaled a fever setting in. She leaned her head back. "I refuse to be sick." She repeated the words three times.

The truck eased forward, and they drove to the home on a rise in a mostly flat landscape. What the land lacked in variation it made up for in immensity. The vistas were exactly what he'd hoped for.

He parked on an expanse of concrete on the left side of the home. A short woman appeared. She looked to be about forty-five years of age and stood in front of his truck. Fen exited and told Bailey to wait for him, and that they'd need to go back to the hotel. Instead of arguing, she closed her eyes in defeat and gave her head a single nod.

"You must be Señor Maguire and Señorita Bailey," said the woman wearing an apron. "I'm sorry J.W. couldn't meet you. He's not well. I tried to call Señora Hope for instructions, but she hasn't returned my call. She was looking forward to you being here, but now that there's sickness, I'm not sure it would be wise."

Fen threw a thumb over his shoulder. "Too late. It hit Bailey a few minutes ago."

"I'm Libby Garza, and I've nursed J.W. back to health all his life. Since everyone is exposed, let's get you and Bailey inside."

"Are you sure?"

"Don't argue. Home is where sick people go to get well, not a hotel. Standing outside in the rain and sleet last night is why they're sick."

Her reply reminded him of Thelma, his housekeeper and cook.

"I got them in my truck as quick as I could last night," said Fen, trying to defend himself.

"Not quick enough. But that's *agua* on the other side of the bridge. Your rooms are ready. I'll get Bailey into pajamas and bed. J.W. has chills and fever. I'm sure Bailey will, too."

Chattering teeth proved the prophecy to be true. Fen passed Bailey over to Libby as he followed behind.

Libby guided Bailey into a bedroom and spoke over her shoulder, "I'll show you to your room as soon as I can. Look around the house if you want to."

The den proved to be a room that fit the ranch motif down to the collection of branding irons mounted on the wall. Photos included a much younger Hope rounding a barrel while riding a horse. Another showed a younger version of J.W. throwing a rope over the head of a calf. Additional family photos showed a tall, well-built man in a cowboy hat alongside Hope and the young, smiling face of J.W. Standing guard over the room was a nine-foot live Christmas tree decorated with everything from tinsel garland to ornaments made in elementary school.

Fen circled the room taking in sculptures and paintings that included the work he'd sold to Hope.

With time to kill, and permission to wander, he stepped

into a home office. The desk was of a tight-grained wood, stained and polished to a gleaming, rich milk-chocolate color. The top of the desk held only the essentials. He concluded Hope was a woman of order. The diploma on the wall confirmed his suspicions about her mental acuity. She held a bachelor of science in organic chemistry.

A voice sounded from behind him. "Señora Hope was going to be an animal doctor, but Señor Ellison had other plans for them."

Instead of asking anything else about the Ellison family, Fen's thoughts went to Bailey. "How's your latest patient?"

"Sick. Chills and fever, the same as J.W. I gave her Tylenol and cold water. She and J.W. must have swapped germs."

"It wouldn't surprise me. She's a good girl, but they're both at that age."

"And he's a good boy," said Libby in a quick response. "I hope they don't get well too quick. How long do you plan on staying?"

The question was one his own housekeeper would ask. Abrupt, pointed, and protective of what she perceived to be her family. He'd need to tread lightly. "My responsibility at MSU lasts only a week. It's Friday, so with any luck we'll be on the road home a week from today."

He didn't mention the case, which might delay their leaving Wichita County indefinitely. If Libby Garza was as perceptive as Thelma, she'd figure it out in the next day or two.

Fen changed the subject. "I understand Hope is coordinating the Christmas parade this year. When is it?"

"A week from tomorrow. Too bad you won't be here to see it."

Fen nodded in agreement. Not because he was sure the case would conclude but because he understood a week would be the limit of Libby's hospitality. Nothing like a little pressure

to get him motivated to solve a case. If things became unbear-
able at Hope's home, he and Bailey could always go back to the
hotel.

In the meantime, he needed to think. His best thinking
came when he painted, but sketching would have to do today.

Chapter Seven

Libby Garza tried to tempt Fen with lunch, but his mind was fixed on the investigation that awaited him. To help him think, he put on his hat and coat and went to the back patio with a sketch pad. Unlike the preceding day's slushy mess of rain and sleet, the weather had cleared. A few contrails from high-flying airplanes marred the otherwise clear, cornflower-blue sky. The scene wasn't one he wanted to paint because it contained a large barn, but it would do for sketching and thinking.

He was adding the weather vane to the top of the barn when his phone interrupted the stillness of the afternoon. He checked the caller's name on the screen. "Hello, Margaret."

"I don't know what you did, but Detective Grimes has a new partner, and I'm assigned to take over the cold case of Regina Cox."

"Is it permanent?"

"The chief told me if I find Regina and recover some of the stolen money, I won't have to work with Detective Grimes."

"Then we'd better get to work."

"Before you get too excited, we need some ground rules. This is my investigation, but the powers that be know I'll be working with you and your team."

"My team is down one. Bailey and J.W. must have cross-contaminated each other. Both are out of commission with flu-like symptoms.

Margaret let a tiny chuckle escape before saying, "The way they were looking at each other, that may be a good thing."

"Hope's housekeeper agrees with you."

"Ah. You met Libby Garza. She can be a little intense."

"Bailey and I are in rooms in one wing of the house, and J.W. is in his room upstairs."

"Libby will probably sleep on the couch at the bottom of the stairs. She's more than a little protective of J.W."

Fen didn't want to belabor the obvious, so he moved on. "How do you want to proceed?"

"Can you come to our ranch this afternoon? Daddy already knows who you are, and he's willing to show you his file."

"I'll put my sketch pad in my room and meet you there. All I need is the address."

She rattled off the physical address and said, "We're the same distance east of town as Hope is on the west."

Once in his truck, he put the address into his trip computer. He turned onto the farm-to-market road and headed toward Wichita Falls. The city was like other cities with a similar population in the vast expanse of the state. A smattering of multi-story buildings existed, but not many. There was no shortage of land in this part of Texas, so the city oozed outward from a center that had seen more prosperous days. Instead of tearing down buildings, it was more cost efficient to let them stand and build new ones a mile or more away. Peaks of construction radiated outward like growth rings on a tree.

Fen took notice of the Wichita River as he passed over it.

The rains had churned up mud that reminded him of a deep burnt-orange color he'd used to paint a sunset some years back. It was an ugly color that spoke of turmoil and danger.

The houses thinned more the farther east he drove until the mailboxes on the side of the road came only every mile or two. He turned onto a well-maintained gravel driveway. The distance from the main road was half that of Hope's, as was the size of the neat brick home with an ample front porch facing southwest.

An arched driveway marked the end of his journey, even though a separate gravel path led around the home. He caught sight of the back half of what he believed was Margaret's unmarked SUV. She met him on the front porch wearing well-worn jeans, a Dallas Cowboys football jersey, and moccasin-style house shoes. Her hair was down. She looked right at home on a ranch.

Fen let his gaze wander over the front of the home as he followed the sidewalk. A fake Christmas tree stood in one corner of the porch, flanked by a light-up Santa. Christmas lights encircled the porch pillars and railing. Chairs sporting snowmen pillows waited for someone to sit a while. As his wife Sally would have said, it was cozy and warm. Something else that set it apart from the Ellison home.

"Come in and meet Daddy. He's still skeptical, but I've softened him up for you."

Fen followed her through the home to the dining room table. Two file folders lay in front of the man, who stood and offered a calloused hand to shake. "Sheriff Maguire," said Margaret's father.

"Sheriff Sibley," said Fen. The two men traded grins as the titles were now honorary.

Fen suggested they call each other by their first names, to which Hap gladly agreed.

"I appreciate you allowing me to look at the work you did on Regina."

"Whoever killed Charley Cleg did the world a favor, but prepare yourself to get frustrated. I don't think the renewed interest in the case is going to help you and Margaret find Regina Cox." Hap settled into a chair and motioned for Fen to sit. He then tilted his head.

Fen took a seat in the first chair next to the head of the table on Hap's left side. The former sheriff of Wichita County pushed the files toward Fen as if he wanted to rid himself of something offensive. Margaret took the seat on her father's right side, opposite Fen.

"I realize it's a long shot that I'll be able to help Margaret find Regina, but I'm willing to try if it helps her career."

Hap reached over and thumped the tall file bulging with papers. "I think you'll find I looked under every rock and behind every bush. I gave up for a while, but Margaret wouldn't let it rest." He tapped on the smaller of the two files. "That's her work."

Margaret spoke next. "All I've done is repeat some interviews. Nothing changed after Daddy ran out of leads."

Fen said, "I work with an investigative reporter and I've got her finding out all she can about Regina Cox. I'll also have her dig into Charley Cleg and see if there's a link between the two."

Hap leaned back with arms crossed over his chest. "She'll be wasting her time. I couldn't find a single person in Wichita Falls who remembers ever seeing Charley and Regina together. Believe me, I looked high and low. One of my theories was, they were in cahoots because he was so detailed in his articles after she disappeared."

Hap took a breath. "Before you ask, I checked phone records on both. No calls between them. Nothing on Regina's computer other than real estate and social events."

Fen needed to make sure he heard Hap's last statement correctly. "Are you saying Regina left her computer for you to find?"

A single nod answered his question.

"Didn't you find that odd? What woman leaves her laptop?"

"Not me," said Margaret. "I'm lost without mine."

Fen wanted to follow up with more questions concerning the computer, but loud knocks on the front door put the discussion on hold.

Hap and Margaret traded glances. He stood. "It might be a good idea if we put the files away."

Margaret didn't waste time. "I'll walk slow and get the door."

Hap sprung from his chair, gathered the folders, and took them out of the room. "I knew Grimes would come by, but I didn't expect him so soon." He returned empty-handed as voices approached.

Detective Grimes appeared with a man wearing a western cut suit in his wake. He carried a black felt cowboy hat in his hand. A generous belly hung over his belt. The follower was perhaps five years younger than the senior detective, which put him in the last third of his career.

Hap didn't rise from his chair to meet them. Fen followed his lead. It was a power move by the two former sheriffs to show who would direct the conversation.

"Hello, Jay. I see you brought Larry with you. That was sure some storm that blew through yesterday. How much rain did you get in town, Larry?"

Fen took note that Hap directed the first question to the junior partner. It was a small insult, but one that hit home with Detective Grimes all the same.

"Uh... I dunno, Sheriff."

Grimes gave his new partner a hard stare and brought his gaze back to Hap, who spoke again before the detective could. "Larry, this is Sheriff Fen Maguire from Newton County. Fen, this is Larry Fry."

Hap sucked in a quick breath and continued, "I heard you were happy staying in uniform. When did you make detective?"

Words came out in a whisper as the man looked down. "It's a temporary assignment. Jay requested I help him with the murder case."

"I'm sure you two will have it wrapped up in the next few days."

Fen noticed that Margaret had gone into the kitchen that overlooked the dining room. All the sounds led to the conclusion she was making a fresh pot of coffee. She spoke over the half wall of the breakfast bar. "Jay, why don't you and Larry take a load off and tell us what's new with your investigation. Anything from the coroner?"

"Someone poisoned him," said Larry before Detective Grimes could speak. This earned the patrolman in plain clothes an unfiltered, icy stare. He seemed to sink into his chair.

Hap sat a little straighter as he turned to Fen. "Poison. Don't you think that's unusual?"

"The only case of poisoning I ever investigated turned out to be accidental. An elderly woman with failing eyesight mistook a box of fire ant poison for baking soda. She had diabetes and couldn't eat sweets, but her husband loved peach pie with Blue Bell vanilla ice cream. The husband had seconds, and it killed him graveyard dead."

Hap broke in. "That's my favorite, but cherry pie will do when peaches are out of season." He launched into a soliloquy about various fruit pies and how he believed vanilla ice cream was the only topping they should receive. Fen glanced at

Detective Grimes when Hap gave his opinion about rhubarb pie. The detective's molars ground.

An explosion seemed imminent until Margaret interrupted with coffee. "Daddy, that's enough talk about pies and ice cream. Unless I'm wrong, Jay and Larry are here on official business."

Hap tilted his head as he finally gave Jay his full attention. "What can I do for you?"

The question was so direct it caught the detective off guard. He recovered enough to say his first words. "I came to talk to both you and Margaret." His gaze shifted to Fen. "Since Mr. Maguire is here, I have some questions for him, too."

"Ask away," said Fen.

The quick response caught the detective on his back foot. He'd lost control of the interview after two sentences.

All eyes were on Detective Grimes as he seemed to regroup. "I need you and that girl to come to my office."

"What girl?"

"Bailey Madison."

"She can't come."

"Why not?"

"She's in bed with the flu. She and I are staying at Hope Ellison's home. Hope's son, J.W., is also sick." He quirked a fake smile. "Call Hope if you need to verify."

Fen ran a hand down his face. "Bailey hasn't had the best experiences with police. I seriously doubt she'll assist you in your investigation without Mrs. Ellison's attorney present."

Detective Grimes puffed up with a full inhale of air. "I can be mighty persuasive once I get someone in an interrogation room."

"Not with Bailey. She's well acquainted with her rights, and she's under no obligation to assist you with your investigation. That limits your options to asking questions through her attorney or asking me."

"Perhaps she'll think otherwise after a few days in jail."

Fen leaned forward. "Are you prepared to arrest J.W. and hold him for questioning? He was in Bailey's room alone, changing into his swimsuit while she went to the pool."

The detective's Adam's apple rose and fell as he swallowed the question that seemed to go down sideways.

Fen kept talking. "I didn't think so." He leaned back in his chair, allowing the tension of the moment to simmer. "I'll fully cooperate with you, but there's nothing to add to my formal statement."

"I'll be the judge of that," said Grimes, once again finding a tablespoon of bravado. "Be at my office tomorrow morning at eight."

"Why not ask me now?"

"I didn't bring your statement."

"Is that the only reason you need me to come tomorrow?"

"Isn't that enough?"

Instead of answering, Fen took out his phone and brought up photos. "This is a picture I took of my statement." He handed his phone to Grimes. "Refresh your memory and ask anything you want."

The detective's eyelids narrowed. "It's too small."

Margaret broke in with a cheerful tone in her voice. "I can help. Email the photo, and I'll run off copies for everyone. I'd like to have a copy for my file."

"Great idea," said Hap. "It's been a while since I've seen a witness statement written by someone who knows what they're doing."

Grimes ignored Hap's contribution. "No copies. Margaret, you're off the murder case, so this doesn't concern you."

Fen focused on Detective Grimes. "I'm still willing to help

you and answer questions, but I don't understand why we can't do it here and now."

Hap piled on. "I'll be your witness to that."

Fen put steel in his next words. "I'll be busy for the foreseeable future helping Detective Sibley with her fraud investigation."

Hap took another turn. "That takes care of Sheriff Maguire. Do you have questions for me?"

"Yeah," said Detective Grimes with frustration seething from his one-word response. "Where were you yesterday afternoon and evening?"

"Here on my ranch."

"Any witnesses?"

"Two, and a video showing my truck never left the driveway."

Officer Fry drew a small notebook from his coat pocket while Grimes demanded, "Names of the witnesses."

"Bartholomew and Ginger. I gave them an extra ration of oats about five o'clock."

Detective Grimes shot up from his seat and stormed out while his new partner lagged behind and asked, "How do you spell Bartholomew?"

"Just put Bart," said Margaret as she walked the officer to the door.

Fen and Hap traded glances and tried without success to stifle their laughter. Margaret returned in a more somber mood. "You two better pray hard that we find Regina. Can you imagine what Jay'll do to me if he's my supervisor again?"

While Hap continued to chuckle, Fen looked at Margaret. "Let's brainstorm a plan to make sure that doesn't happen. Get the files and let's get started. I'm glad you made coffee. It may be a long night."

Chapter Eight

Daybreak on Saturday morning found Fen once again in a hotel's restaurant. Libby, worn thin from caring for Bailey and J.W., all but threw him out of the house. One thing she didn't want was one more person with the flu or whatever afflicted her patients.

She strongly encouraged him to spend as little time as possible in Hope's home. Whatever had attacked the youngsters showed no signs of abating. Neither of them could keep water down and the soup Libby made was out of the question. Their fevers spiked at 103 before over-the-counter meds and cold compresses brought them down to the high 90s. Chills had their teeth chattering before the fever broke and soaked their sheets with sweat. Diarrhea made its unwelcome visit during the night.

Fen didn't need to be told twice. The first pink streaks shot from the eastern sky as he drove to wait for Lou to come to life.

The ringing of his phone sounded as he raised the day's first cup of coffee. He closed his eyes and groaned when he saw the name of the caller. Five rings later, he knew it wouldn't stop until he answered. "Good morning, Thelma."

"Don't you 'good morning' me. What's wrong with Bailey?"

"She's sick. How did you find out?"

He knew it was a foolish question. Thelma stayed in daily contact with Bailey and Lou whenever they were out of town. That went double if they were helping him with a case.

"Don't you worry 'bout how I know things. How sick is she?"

"It's not pretty. High fever, vomiting and diarrhea."

"What about chills?"

"Those, too."

"What did the doctor say?"

"Uhh..."

Fen sensed Thelma's pressure rising like a volcano spewing hot gas before an eruption. He tried to head it off. "She's in capable hands and is being looked after twenty-four hours a day."

"I know it's not you or Lou nursing her. Who is it?"

She'd trapped him like a fly in a spider's web. His next answer would seal his fate. "It's a long story, and I don't have time to—"

"Then make it short. If she's in a hotel room knocking on death's door, I'm coming to fetch her."

Fen didn't know where to start, so he picked a spot and talked fast. "When we came in September, she met a young man. A very nice young man whose family owns a ranch that makes my four thousand acres look like a postage stamp on a large envelope. Someone murdered a man in the hotel room next door to Bailey's. I was asleep when the smoke alarm went off. Bailey and J.W.—that's her sort-of-boyfriend—were in the swimming pool when the police and firefighters came and evac-uated the building. It was raining and sleeting and they had to stand outside until the firefighters discovered it was only a bag of popcorn that caught fire in a microwave. Anyway, that's when they discovered the dead man."

"Have you been drinkin'?"

Fen ignored her question and plowed on. "The police wouldn't let Bailey in her room because it has a door that adjoins the room of the dead man and is part of the crime scene. J.W.'s mother, her name is Hope Ellison, she's a big wig around here and invited us to stay with her. J.W. is upstairs in his room, and Bailey and I have our own rooms in a separate wing of the house. The housekeeper and cook, Libby Garza, is taking care of J.W. and Bailey."

Silence filled the air for so long that Fen had to check his phone to make sure the connection was still good. Thelma finally spoke, "You've only been gone two days. How'd you get in such a mess so fast?"

"I'm guessing you don't want to hear about the case Lou and I are working on with a former sheriff and his daughter, who's a police detective."

Thelma's next words sounded like she chipped them from a block of granite. "I have my bags packed and I'm coming. That woman looking after Bailey and J.W. must be worn to a nub. Dealing with two people suffering from double-buckets is no bargain. She needs help, and Bailey can't count on you. Send me the address. I'll be there quick as I can."

Fen knew better than to argue. The best thing for him to do was thank her, hang up, and call Hope. He wondered how she'd take the news of another visitor, but he needn't have worried.

"Libby told me she showed you the door. She's grumpier than usual after a double shift on the bedpan brigade."

She went on after a quick breath. "I had my next-door neighbor stop by on the way to complete his hospital rounds this morning. He checked on both patients. It's not the flu, but a nasty virus. It has to run its course, which usually takes a week."

"That's why I called," said Fen. "My housekeeper, Thelma, volunteered to come and lend a hand. In fact, she downright insisted on it. I hope you don't mind. She's like a momma bear with Bailey."

"It sounds like they cut Thelma and Libby from the same cloth. As for her coming, you took something off my plate that I didn't want to deal with. I was on the verge of hiring a nurse."

The call ended, and Fen wondered how Libby and Thelma would get along. Both seemed overly protective of their cub. He concluded by telling himself not to fret about the possibility of conflict between the two headstrong women. There were plenty of other things to think about.

He nursed his coffee until Lou joined him. She eased into the booth and sat opposite him. Fen gave her a sideways glance. "Would you happen to know how Thelma found out Bailey is sick as a dog that ate a box of chocolate-covered cherries?"

Lou had her hair piled on her head in a messy bun. She crossed her arms over her chest. "I plead the fifth. Did Thelma leave bite marks when she chewed on you?"

"She may when she gets here."

"When she gets here?"

"She invited herself to take care of Bailey. I pity the highway patrolman who pulls her over for speeding."

Lou poured herself a cup of coffee from the carafe the server left on the table. "Have you warned Mrs. Ellison about Thelma?"

He nodded. "Her cook and housekeeper is a bilingual version of Thelma named Libby Garza. She worked through the night cleaning puke and spraying Lysol. J.W. and Bailey are competing to see who's sickest. Hope didn't decline the help."

"Yuk." Lou took her first sip of coffee. "Libby and Thelma should get along until their patients recover. I don't care how big Mrs. Ellison's home is, there won't be enough room for both of them under one roof."

He agreed with a quick nod. "I hope you're well rested. I need you to go to the TIMES RECORD NEWS office and find everything you can on Regina Cox and Charley Cleg."

Lou looked over the top of her upraised cup. "I went there when I arrived in town yesterday afternoon. I stayed until they threw me out and got a good jump on collecting information on Regina Cox. She made quite a splash with the upper crust of Wichita Falls."

"Can you go back today?"

"After one o'clock. It's Sunday and this city must be the buckle of the bible belt. The newspaper has a deal with God that nothing newsworthy can happen until after church." She shifted her gaze to a bleary-eyed couple with two young children in fleece pajamas. "Don't worry. I have plenty of things I can search for online this morning."

"Me, too," said Fen. He told her about the meeting he had with the former sheriff and Margaret Sibley. Lou finished two cups of coffee as he relayed the previous day's exploits.

"What's your read on Hap?"

"He's about my age, a few years older than you. A widower. He and his daughter seem honest and hardworking. She's fighting the good old boys at the city police department. Hap's trying to get over not being sheriff. Charley put a big torpedo in his career."

"What's he doing now?"

"Some sort of regional emergency preparedness coordinator. It's not full time, and I could tell it's not what he wants to do, but he's well qualified. He also has a ranch that keeps him busy."

Lou released a whispered, "Huh."

"What's that supposed to mean?"

She folded her hands on the table behind her coffee cup. "I asked about Hap, and you told me about him and his daughter. Is she pretty?"

Fen's shoulders twitched. "I guess. She's also a couple of decades younger than me and intent on making a name for herself in her career."

He rested his elbows on the table and his chin on his knuckles. "That was a good try, but there's no smoke, let alone a fire, in the romance department. You know I'm a one-woman man, even though Sally's been gone for quite a while."

"Just checking," said Lou through a mischievous smile.

"If you want to talk to someone about romance, ask Bailey after she recovers from her creeping crud."

"Do you think she's serious about J.W.?"

"Like everything else, there's not enough information at this point to make a determination."

Lou seemed to receive the information, and moved on without comment. "What are the chances of me getting access to Hap's file? There has to be some juicy information in it."

Fen wiggled his eyebrows. "He's a widower. You're a lonely divorcée. You should be able to talk him into letting you have a peek."

"Not interested, and certainly not funny."

"The thought of husband number four doesn't intrigue you?"

A manufactured shiver coursed through Lou. "I'll get a gun and do myself in before I sign another wedding license. Besides, he sounds like a carbon copy of you."

"Don't be so quick to judge. We're taking Hap and Margaret out for supper tonight. If you want to have access to their files, you'll have to be on your best behavior."

Lou moaned. "Please tell me we're not going to a nice restaurant. I really don't want to shave my legs."

"Too late. It's heels and hose for you, Margaret, and Hope. She and I are staying away from the quarantine area."

"That's not so bad. At least I won't be stuck acting like I'm interested in what a former sheriff has to say about the price of cattle."

The server came and they ordered breakfast. Lou passed her menu back to the server and faced Fen. "What are you doing today?"

"This morning I'm staying here and finding out all I can about several suspects in the murder investigation. Hope gave me the names."

"I thought this was a missing person investigation. When did it turn into finding Charley's killer?"

"We may have to solve a murder in order to discover what happened to Regina Cox. That's why I have an appointment to speak to Charley's ex-wife today. Her name is Lisa Stuart. She took her maiden name back when they divorced."

"Was that before or after Regina disappeared?"

"That's one thing I want to discover before I drive to Fort Worth to see her."

"Will you be able to make it back in time for supper?"

"That's the plan. If I'm late, you'll need to carry the conversation."

She let out a short, "Thanks. Nothing like a little pressure."

"You're the one who chose a career with deadlines. Pressure makes you happy."

"Not when it involves a crusty ex-sheriff. Present company included."

Chapter Nine

By eight o'clock Fen had gleaned what he could from the file concerning Lisa Stuart. His appointment with her wasn't until eleven, and it was only a two-hour drive from Wichita Falls to Fort Worth.

After some light digging on the internet, he learned she lived in a posh golf course community on the banks of Eagle Mountain Lake. That put her even closer to Wichita Falls.

With an hour and some change to kill, he went to Lucy Park on the banks of the Wichita River in search of the famous falls. His jacket stayed zipped up to ward off a cool wind as he followed a pair of signs that read *WICHITA RIVER TRAIL* and *THE FALLS*. A half-mile later, he'd reached his destination. True to its name, the muddy water tumbling down came from the Wichita River.

The joke, however, was on the unwary visitor. The falls were man-made. Pumps brought rust-colored water to the top of a steep river bank where it tumbled down a series of quarried stones and flowed back into the river.

How many travelers take a brief detour on their way across

the country, expecting to see a natural waterfall? A better question came to him. Who named the city after a non-existent waterfall in the first place? Was it a joke? An attempt to deceive? Fen turned to retrace his steps to his truck. No matter; there were more important things to consider and an interview to conduct.

The weather and traffic both cooperated. Mile after mile slipped by as he rolled down a well-maintained, four-lane highway. The voice from his truck's GPS didn't have to give many instructions before he approached the turnoff to Eagle Mountain Lake. He followed the commands of a female artificial intelligence voice until it announced, "You've arrived at your destination." The solid-looking home in a golfing community fit in well with its upper-middle-class neighbors.

Except for the walk along the river, he'd been sitting all morning. The clock on the truck's dashboard read eleven o'clock. He stepped out of the truck and stretched.

Following a concrete sidewalk, he mounted steps to the front porch and rang the doorbell. As he waited, he took in the tasteful, but subdued Christmas decor. When the door opened, he took off his Stetson. "Ms. Stuart?"

The woman wasn't smiling. "If you're half as rude as those two idiot cops that left an hour ago, you can turn around and go back to Wichita Falls."

He held up his hands. "I'm not a cop, and I'm only visiting Wichita Falls. Please don't sic the dogs on me. I'm not even trying to sell you anything." He paused and gave the most boyish grin he could produce on short notice.

Perhaps it was his calm demeanor, the words he used, or the smile, but something took the venom out of her voice. "Sorry," she said. "Someone needs to teach that Detective Grimes some manners."

She gave him a boot-to-hair inspection. "You'd better come

in so we can get this over with. If you hadn't been so nice when you called, I'd never have agreed to talk to you."

She spun on the heel of her cross-trainers while motioning him to follow. Black leggings and a form-fitting workout top showed off a well-proportioned figure. A quick scan revealed a woman who spent a considerable amount of time on her appearance. The words plucked, painted, powdered, and perfumed came to mind.

He scanned the decor of the home. It communicated wealth and style. Her Christmas tree looked like a professional decorator had been here. This thirty-something woman was enjoying the benefits of someone's labor. Was it hers? He doubted it. The morning's research showed she'd spent three years in college but never graduated. She was a year younger than Charley and the marriage had produced no children.

"You have a beautiful home, Ms. Stuart."

"Call me Lisa, and thanks. I like it."

A glance out the rear-facing living room windows revealed a tastefully landscaped backyard with a wooden privacy fence. What looked like a gate connected Lisa's backyard to the yard of the home behind her. Fen tilted his head. "Is there a story about the gate in the fence?"

"You're very observant. The home behind this one was owned by the brother of the man who lived here. They put a gate in so they wouldn't have to go around the block to visit. It stays locked now."

Lisa floated into a chair and motioned for him to follow her lead but on a loveseat facing her. She opened the conversation. "You said you're after information on Regina Cox."

"Correct. I also suggested you do a computer search if you wanted to know about me. Did you?"

Her ponytail bobbed. "Quite impressive. Ten years as a state trooper, ten years as a sheriff, and a well-respected artist. If you're investigating a crime, why not Charley's murder?"

"That's a recent event that the police are handling. Also, it seems the people in Wichita Falls are more interested in Regina than they are in Charley."

"I didn't get that impression from the detective that left a half hour ago. He never mentioned Regina, but he hammered away at the percentage of women who kill their ex-husbands. I think he made up the statistics."

"I've found it's the current wife who's most likely to kill her husband. Why get rid of someone who's already gone?"

"That makes sense. I told them to find Charley's latest fling. I left him for greener pastures a long time ago."

Fen wiggled the fingers of his left hand. "I see you're not wearing a wedding band. Was one marriage all you could stand?"

She graced him with a coy smile. "Let's say I'm not opposed to the idea, but I'll be a lot more discerning next time." She mimicked the wiggling of the fingers of her left hand. "You still wear a ring."

"I'm fending off the thousands of women who keep throwing themselves before me."

This earned a genuine laugh. She gave him a closer look. "No. You wear it because you're not on the market. I've been single long enough to tell when a man's not ready to play the dating game."

Fen needed to move on before visions of Sally came calling and he lost his train of thought. He said the first thing that popped into his mind. "How long since your divorce was final?"

"I thought you were interested in Regina."

"I am. I wondered if your husband's obsession with investigating Regina put a strain on your marriage."

Her answer came with certainty. "We were having prob-lems long before she arrived in Wichita Falls."

"So, Regina wasn't in Wichita Falls while you were living there?"

"I moved before she arrived. Of course, when Charley wrote his articles exposing the big scam, everything changed for him. The big newspapers in Dallas and Fort Worth thought he was the next big thing in investigative reporters. After he did his best to destroy reputations, he moved to Fort Worth."

"Why did he recently return to Wichita Falls?"

She slowly crossed her left leg over her right. "I'm not the one who's good at solving crimes. You tell me."

He considered dodging the question but thought better of it. The seed of a theory sprouted in his mind and this seemed as good a time as any to see how it sounded. "If I was trying to solve his murder, I'd explore the possibility that someone lured him back. Perhaps they had an ax to grind."

That possibility seemed a stretch, but he kept talking, "Here's another possibility. Charley discovered another victim of Regina's scam that he'd missed. It would need to be a person with a high profile. Someone with a lot to lose. That person turned the tables on him and killed him the day he checked into the hotel."

Lisa leaned forward, her head nodding in agreement. "That sounds like the type of bait Charley would fall for. He'd do anything to get a juicy follow-up story. It would allow him to dredge up the old story and breathe new life into it. He'd milk it for at least a three-part series."

"How was his career after he left Wichita Falls?"

"Never the same. The phrase one-hit-wonder comes to mind."

The interview was going better than he expected, but he

needed to shake things up to keep her talking. "Are you hungry?"

"Starving. All I had for breakfast was a protein shake."

"Can I take you to lunch? My breakfast left me as I passed through Decatur."

She looked down at her attire. "If you don't mind being seen with me looking like this in public, I'm ready and willing."

He wondered if the last thought was innocent or had a double meaning. He played along. "You'll do just fine."

"The clubhouse serves a decent lunch, if you like pub-grub and don't mind talk of golf."

He responded with a nod.

She rose and stretched. "The course is still too wet for golf carts. Most of the residents in this community are retired and don't like to walk from the cart path to where they hit their ball. That adds up to a meager lunch crowd."

"Perfect. Grab your coat."

The short drive didn't give him much time to arrange his thoughts. A question kept niggling his mind, but he wasn't sure how to ask it. Up to now, Lisa had shown no sign of mourning the sudden death of her former husband.

Possibilities flashed like balls of fire from a Roman candle. Perhaps their relationship never was very good. That didn't ring true. She'd left college for him with only a year remaining.

She pointed in the directions he needed to turn. He made small talk about the neighborhood and faked interest in her responses.

Perhaps she married for love, but the pressure from Charley's job as a reporter cooled the relationship until it died a slow death. He wondered what kind of work she did when they were married and if her job contributed to the rift.

Had Charley known Regina before she moved to Wichita

Falls? Of all the mental guesswork, this seemed the most unlikely, but it was worth exploring.

"I told you it wasn't far," said Lisa as he parked in a lot with an abundance of empty striped spaces. "I'm so glad you invited me. We'll have tongues wagging, for sure."

Lisa's gaze remained straight in front of her. Fen took in the reaction of people as they walked through the retail shop and into the restaurant and bar aptly named THE 19TH HOLE. Her presence turned the heads of the patrons. Not surprising since most people in the shop and restaurant were male and looked old enough to have a Medicare card in their wallet. Once seated, she ordered a mimosa while Fen told the server he'd have iced tea.

His scan of the room took in more details. He nodded in approval. "So this is what retirement looks like."

Lisa's head tilted to one side. "Are you a golfer?"

"I heard a quote about golfing. I believe it was one of the past presidents who made it. He said playing golf was a good way to ruin a walk."

She leaned forward and cupped her hand as if hiding a secret from eavesdroppers. "It's not the golf that people hate, it's all the walking. That's why everyone owns a golf cart."

"Including you?"

The question resulted in her showing off ultra-white teeth. "It's pink and made to look like a Rolls Royce."

The server arrived with drinks, which put the conversation on hold as they ordered their meal. It came as no surprise when Lisa ordered a wedge salad. He decided a chef salad was all he needed since he'd had a full breakfast and a steak awaited him for supper.

"Watching your weight?" asked Lisa.

"More like watching it go up since Thanksgiving."

He reminded himself to get down to business. "How would you describe your marriage to Charley?"

The question didn't seem to throw Lisa off her game. "Like so many other failed marriages, mutual attraction and wild passion marked our college experience. He was going to stick around and start grad school while I finished my degree. I wanted to be a pharmacist."

She gave a rueful laugh. "You would have thought a future pharmacist would have known how not to get pregnant."

"Ah," said Fen.

"Yeah. 'Ah.'" She took a long drink before continuing her story. "Charley insisted on doing the honorable thing and we were married before I started showing. We lost the baby on our honeymoon."

Fen's hands involuntarily clenched and released. "I'm sorry. I can't imagine how hard that was for both of you."

A distant look came into Lisa's eyes. "We both changed. I acted like a turtle and pulled into my shell. It took a full year for me to act like a wife again. Charley's change was more gradual. He transitioned from a fun-loving optimist into a man with a chip on his shoulder the size of a giant sequoia."

Lisa returned her gaze to him. "I realize now that his job had a lot to do with it. They pay newspaper reporters to write about conflict. Exposing injustice and greedy people making money off the misery of others consumed him. He'd do anything to get stories like that."

Fen offered a sympathetic nod to show he was tracking. "That must have taken a toll on your marriage."

"I liken his obsession to a cancer that eventually killed our love. It wasn't a bitter divorce; more like a slow death."

"And all this happened before Regina moved to Wichita Falls?"

A nod sufficed for an answer, but she added, "Regina's

scam must have been like cocaine to Charley's addiction to right the wrongs of society."

Her voice took on a dismissive tone. "I'd moved on before his obsession destroyed me along with him."

Their salads arrived, which put a temporary hold on further questions. As the meal progressed, Fen wondered how to broach a delicate subject.

Lisa must have sensed his discomfort. She leaned forward. "If I was in your shoes, I'd wonder where this woman in front of me got the money needed to live this lifestyle." Her eyebrows lifted. "Am I right?"

He released a sigh of relief. "I'm losing my touch. I was much more direct when I was a cop."

Lisa continued without prompting, "The money came from an inheritance. It's amazing what a difference hundreds of thousands of dollars can make."

He thought it unusual that she'd volunteered the information. The trip back to Wichita Falls would give him time to process their meeting. A frequently quoted adage by another former president came to mind. "Trust, but verify."

Fen lightened the remainder of their conversation with talk of her experience in a golf community. The longer he stayed in the restaurant, the more apparent it became that not all the patrons were older and most knew her by name.

After the meal, he dropped her at her home. His thoughts had already shifted to the questions he'd need to ask Hope at supper. He also thought of the thick steak he'd order.

Chapter Ten

The restaurant Hope chose was what Fen expected. It boasted crisp, white tablecloths along with a full complement of silverware. The room's carpet muffled the sound of conversations as classical music set the mood. Servers, both male and female, wore white shirts under black jackets. Coal-colored slacks and polished black shoes completed the ensembles.

Fen and Hope arrived together, as did Margaret and her father, Hap. Lou breezed in five minutes later, looking rushed, as usual. "Sorry," she said. "I'm finding the older I get, the longer it takes to look presentable."

Fen took care of introductions. He added a piece of Lou's biography. "Lou was a reporter for the major newspaper in Dallas before moving to Newton County."

Hap responded to her vocation by looking as if he'd taken a bite out of a lemon. Lou caught his look of disdain, but held her peace. She must have been in a benevolent mood. Holding her tongue didn't come naturally.

Hope played hostess. "Fen, thank you for suggesting this gathering. I trust no one is in a hurry to leave tonight. Shall we start with drinks?" She motioned to a server. "I don't know about the rest of you, but after the day I had, bourbon on the rocks is required."

Hope repeated her order to the young server.

"Put a splash of water in mine," said Hap. "Make sure they don't drown it. If we're going to talk about you-know-who, I need snake-bite medicine."

Lou spoke next. "I'll take a whiskey sour." She looked at Hap with a sideways glance. "I've been told it fits my personality."

Margaret went next. "Beer on tap. Whatever you come to first."

"Same for me," said Fen, even though he rarely drank alcohol and knew he'd do well to get half of it down.

Fen cast his gaze to Hope. "Rough day?"

"It would have been rougher if your housekeeper hadn't come to lend a hand. J.W. is as sick as I've ever seen him. I don't have time to get whatever he has, so I'm staying away as much as possible."

"Thelma said something similar about Bailey. She told me to stay out of your home unless I was sleeping or changing clothes."

Hap directed his first question to Hope. "Any changes with the Christmas parade this year?"

Hope released a strangled breath. "I'm now having to play arbitrator with the battle of the believers. Every church has their own idea of where they need to be in the parade, which is as close to the front as they can get. The pastors and priests have sense enough not to get directly involved. They deputized surrogates to wrangle for positions."

"Any bloodshed?" asked Hap.

"Not yet, but it's a good thing dagger stares don't count."

Lou shook her head in disgust, so Fen moved off the subject before she said something to offend the locals. "How did your research go today, Lou?"

"Disappointing and surprising at the same time."

"How so?"

"It had to do with my research on Regina Cox. Normally, it takes people years to fit into the fabric of a city this size. Regina was involved in women's organizations and clubs in mere months. She must've had an amazing ability to remember names."

"She did," said Hope. "And it wasn't just names. It was like she studied the city and county for years before she moved here. Almost as if she was born here."

Margaret chimed in. "She knew when mom died, even though it was years before." She looked at Fen. "I never thought of that before today."

"I did," said Hap. "She came with a scheme that must have taken her more than a year to plan. Looking back on things, she knew way too many details about people's lives and knew just what to say."

Their drinks arrived, and not a moment too soon. The unpleasant memories of Regina left a cloud over the group. Fen wondered how many wished they'd ordered doubles.

The server moved away, and Margaret turned to Fen, "Did you learn anything new today with Lisa Stuart?"

"Some, but I don't think it'll bring us any closer to finding Regina. I wasn't expecting her to live in a golf course community next to Eagle Mountain Lake."

Hap came on point. "When and where did she get that kind of money? The last time I checked, she had a one-bedroom place in Fort Worth."

"She told me she came into a substantial inheritance."

Hap nodded. "That's possible. Her father had heart problems."

Hope asked, "How much inheritance are we talking about?"

"Multiple hundreds of thousands. She wasn't specific."

Margaret took out a small spiral notebook. "I'll check on that, just to update the file."

"What file?" asked Lou.

Fen quickly jumped in. "Margaret started a file on Regina."

Lou looked like a hound who'd caught a fresh scent. Fen wanted Lou to look at the investigation with fresh eyes, starting with the newspaper articles. His plan was to breach the topic of Hap and Margaret allowing Lou access to their files later.

Lou put her glass down and looked at Margaret. "I have plenty to keep me busy for several days, but when I run out of things to do, I'd like to see your file."

Hap shook his head. "You can forget that idea."

"Why?" snapped Lou. "I thought you wanted to find Regina. You've looked for years with no success."

Hap gave Lou a narrow-eyed squint. "Those are official police documents. If what's in them appears in print, it could cost my daughter her job. I know you reporters don't care about things like that, but it matters to me."

Fen had to act, or the supper would end in a shouting match. "Why don't we all take a step back and look at the big picture?"

"I need another whiskey sour," said Lou.

Hope held up her empty glass, as did Hap and Margaret.

"We're making progress," said Fen. "Four out of five need another drink."

Hap grumbled and turned to Margaret. "Not you, honey. You're driving tonight. I've got a feeling this meeting will require a fair amount of lubrication."

Fen took a full drink from his mug. Hap may have spoken an accurate prophecy. An idea of how to proceed occurred to him. "In my career in law enforcement, I discovered that most disagreements start because people want different things."

"What are you getting at?" asked Lou.

"What do each of us hope to accomplish by finding out where Regina is?"

Lou was the first to respond. "You already know why I follow you all over the state. You use me for research, and I get interesting stories I can sell to news outlets. The stories will someday go into books that will supplement my retirement."

Hap snorted out his nose and mumbled. "Reporters."

Lou returned the snort. "Former sheriffs! At least I'm still working and earning a living. What are you doing now?"

Fen didn't allow him time to respond. "What about you, Hope? Why are you interested in finding Regina?"

She looked up from her empty glass. "So many people lost money. I want to get some of it back for them."

"What else?" asked Fen in a softer voice.

"Reputations. People like Hap, Mason Cleg, and Cleo Clayton lost what money can't buy."

"Don't forget to add yourself to that list."

Lou, ever inquisitive, asked, "Who are Mason Cleg and Cleo Clayton?"

Margaret shifted her gaze to Lou. "Mason is Charley's brother; it cost him his marriage and children. Cleo was the vice president of the bank that provided much of the financing for Regina's deals. She was the scapegoat for the decisions the board of directors made."

Hap shook his head. "I hate to admit it, but I came down way too hard on Cleo. Charley's articles had so many details I was sure she had something to do with Regina."

Lou leaned forward as she took in every word. "I read a few

of Charley's articles. They seemed slanted to put most of the blame on Regina, but he pulled no punches with her victims. It was as if he wanted to punish everyone."

Fen filed that comment away. Lou could not only write the lines, but she could read between them. It made sense that Charley would blame Regina, but why attack her victims?

He moved on. "Margaret, your turn. Why is it so important to you that Regina pays for her sins?"

"It's my job."

"True, but that's not all."

She interlaced her fingers. "It's what we've said so far, especially the part about reputations. I saw what it did to Daddy, and I want him to get back to acting like the man I know him to be—the one who holds his head high and keeps his shoulders back."

Margaret seemed to look longingly into the future. "Slapping handcuffs on Regina would be the highlight of my career." She tilted her head. "You're the only one left, Sheriff Maguire. What's your motivation?"

He grinned. "The same as Superman's... truth, justice, and the American way."

When the laughter subsided, Lou said, "Don't expect to get straight answers out of him. I'm not sure he knows why he likes to solve the crimes others can't."

Fen didn't dispute her assessment. "I think it's for the same reason I paint. I like to do it. Solving a crime comes with its own rewards."

Heads bobbed as he kept talking. "Now that we have a better idea of our motivations for finding Regina, let's have a pleasant meal."

"My treat," said Hope.

"I'll flip you for the bill," said Fen. "I'm having the biggest steak they offer."

"No matter. All the beef cooked in this restaurant comes from my ranch."

"In that case, I hope you win the coin toss."

The clarification of motives seemed to take the edge off further discussions about Regina and Charley. Anecdotes about the missing woman and the man who added insult to injury flew across the table. The addition of a third round of drinks before they ordered added to the quantity of words. Even Hap didn't seem to mind that Lou scribbled notes.

The servers took orders, and Hope excused herself to powder her nose. Fen enjoyed the newfound sense of bonhomie among the group. They were a diverse group, each with their own reasons for wanting to apprehend Regina, but that desire was the glue that bound them together.

Hope had no more left the room when Detective Grimes and his officer-shadow entered. He scanned the tables, ignored the hostess's attempt to seat him, and cut a path to their table. It didn't take long for Grimes to cover the distance. He scanned the faces of those assembled, stopping at Lou. He'd recognized everyone else.

"Sorry to interrupt," said Grimes, without a hint of regret in his voice. He shifted his gaze to Hap. "Mr. Sibley, I've been calling you."

"I turned my phone off. What do you want?"

"Answers to questions."

"Come see me tomorrow."

Fen could see the two men were squaring off for a verbal shoot-out. He didn't want the evening spoiled but wasn't sure how to avoid a scene. It was too late. Lou had her phone in hand and pointed it at Detective Grimes. He reacted as expected, with overreaction.

"Put it up, lady. You can't film me."

"I'm a reporter, and I certainly can film you. There's a document called the Bill of Rights that gives me permission."

"In public. This is private property."

Lou wasn't one to back down. "There's nothing posted that prohibits it; therefore, it's legal." She gave him a slow shake of her head. "You really should brush up on the laws pertaining to where filming is permitted."

He pulled back his sports coat to reveal the badge on his belt. "This says if you keep filming me, I'll arrest you for disturbing the peace."

Lou stood with her phone extended toward him. Grimes might as well have waved a red flag in front of her.

Margaret stayed seated but spoke in a firm voice, "You're out of line, Jay. She's right. The only way she's prohibited from filming is if the owner or manager tells her she can't."

Carpet muffled Hope's footfalls as she approached the table from behind the surly detective. "Jay Grimes, I don't know who put a burr under your blanket, but don't make me call the chief and tell him you made a fool of yourself."

Lou kept filming. "Look around, Detective. Half the people in the room have their phones out. The days of cops trying to bully their way past the Constitution are at an end. What are you going to do? Falsely arrest everyone filming?"

Fen cast his gaze to the tables where several phones pointed their way.

The bravado leaked from Detective Grimes like he was a rotten rowboat, but he needed to save face. With rich sarcasm, he bowed at the waist. "Please forgive an old, ignorant cop. Former Sheriff Sibley, if you'd be so kind as to call me tomorrow morning, I'd like to converse with you about a small legal matter. It seems a man died as the result of poisoning. The poison matches what you recently purchased."

The two officers of the law left. Margaret's gaze rested on her father. "Daddy, have you been poisoning coyotes again?"

He gave a sheepish response, "I know you like to shoot 'em, but you've been so busy lately. They killed a calf this past week, and I can't abide by that."

Hope added, "Half the ranchers in the county use poison to thin out the coyotes. That tells me Grimes is grasping at straws."

Their food arrived and exclamations of pleasure replaced talk of death. After the first few bites, Hope turned her attention to Fen. "Tomorrow's Monday, your first day at the college. What will you have the students do?"

"Not much. I'll make myself available all day if they want to talk to me."

Lou reached for her drink but didn't lift it. "What if no one needs help or wants to talk to you?"

"That's even better. I'll have a day to paint and think."

Hope asked, "Is that how you solve crimes?"

Fen continued cutting a bite of steak. "Now you know my secret."

The surprise of the night came when Fen noticed Lou and Hap had replaced suspicious glares with looks of interest. Perhaps opposites really attract.

Hope caught his eye, and gave an almost imperceptible wink and nod toward the unlikely couple, confirming his suspicions.

Chapter Eleven

F en found himself once again in the hotel's restaurant, sipping coffee. Thelma had told him to get out of Hope's home without delay this morning. The virus showed modest signs of abating. Bailey and J.W. made less frequent trips to the bathrooms, but their woes lingered on. Even Thelma's top-secret home remedy hadn't offered relief. It was a blow to her ego. The only consolation was that Libby's concoction hadn't done J.W. any good either.

Lou arrived ten minutes later, looking the worse for wear with puffy eyes and hair stuffed under a baseball cap. Not wanting to start her day off on a sour note, he decided not to ask her why she looked so bedraggled. Instead, he started the conversation with an open-ended question. "Short night?"

Lou groaned out a quick "Uh-huh."

"Did you work on the case?"

She shook her head. "Remind me I'm not as young as I used to be."

"Too many whiskey sours?"

"Too little sleep. Hap and I went to an all-night coffee shop for dessert. I have a peach pie and ice cream hangover."

"Did you get him talking? He seems like a man of few words."

"Don't let him fool you. There are plenty of words in him. No nice ones about Regina Cox or Charley Cleg, but plenty about his daughter. I don't know if I've ever met a man so proud of his little girl."

Fen slipped his finger into the handle of his coffee cup. "There's a lot to be proud of. She'll follow in his footsteps one day and become the sheriff of this county or the chief of police. Mark my words."

Lou tilted her head. "Even with the stain on the family name?"

Fen considered the question as he took a sip from the porcelain cup and returned it to the table. "If we do our job, there won't be a stain anymore." He leaned back. "Is it another day at the newspaper for you?"

"Monday means another work week. I'll put in a full day."

"Do you want to meet tonight and compare notes?"

"Not tonight, if you don't mind."

He wiggled his eyebrows. "You must have scored a better offer."

She cast her gaze away from his. "I'm hoping to get a look at what's in Margaret's file."

Her response didn't surprise him, but he sensed he'd better not tease about her personal life. Three marriages had burned her, and it was a miracle she was on speaking terms with the former sheriff. Best to back off and let nature take its course.

Fen checked the time on his phone. "I need to run. Don't want to be late for my first day of classes. Good luck with your research. Call if you find anything important."

"Are you planning to stay on campus all day?"

He stood, lifted his shoulders, and let them fall. "There're only two classes, and it's a dead week with finals on Friday. I'll probably paint and think this afternoon."

A ten-minute drive brought him to the campus of MSU where he found the art studio with no problem. Some twenty students filed in, most looking like they'd enjoyed the weekend and needed to catch up on sleep. Lou would have fit in well with this group.

He looked at the class roster but didn't call roll. These were adults who paid to attend. If they skipped, that was their business. A deep voice sounded from the back row. "What are we doing today?"

"Your professor said you can review, use the time to study for your final exam or complete your projects. If you don't want to do any of those things, I'll be glad to blab for fifty minutes."

The baritone voice boomed again. "I hear you're a big-time painter. Why don't you tell us your secrets to making a good living?"

"Don't pay any attention to Dave," said a girl in the second row. She had a silver bar through her nose, St. Patrick's Day green hair, and a spiderweb tattoo on her neck.

"It's all about the money," said Dave, in a cocky voice. "Teach us in less than an hour how to get rich being an artist."

Two other voices chimed in to repeat the challenge. The only question was how to respond. Fen noticed large sketch pads on easels lining the walls. "All right, Dave. I'll show you how I paid my way through college and spent the first five years after I graduated while I worked as a state trooper."

"You were a cop?"

"You dunce," said the same girl. "If you hadn't slept through class, you'd know he was a highway patrolman and a sheriff."

"Come up here, Dave. You and I are going to have a contest. How are you at drawing caricatures?"

"The best in town."

"Are you fast?"

Dave pretended to draw a pistol. "The fastest pencils on either side of the Red River."

"Can you complete a three-color caricature of me in ten minutes?"

"Let's make it eight. Amateurs need ten minutes."

The green-haired young lady rose and went to a cabinet. "I'll get the pencils. This is going to be good. Smoke him, Mr. Maguire."

Fen took over. "We'll each have eight minutes to complete and sign a caricature of the other. The class will decide the winner. If either of us finishes before the allotted time, there's extra credit."

"How much?"

"Five points for every thirty seconds." He turned to the class. "Twenty points each for originality, composition, shading, detail, and storytelling. Extra points for speed."

The students made notes of the criteria used to arrive at a grade. Fen and Dave faced each other at angles that didn't allow them to see each other's work and mostly blocked the class from seeing.

Fen said, "We need someone to keep time. Holler out every minute."

"Everyone has a phone, so we'll all do it," came a voice from the front row.

Dave took a pencil in hand and pointed it at Fen. "You're going down, old man."

Fen grinned. "That's big talk from a man wearing pajamas."

The green-haired woman raised her hand. "Is everyone ready?"

Heads bobbed.

"On three: One... two... go!"

The only sound in the room was pencils dragging against paper. Fen had already committed Dave's face and frame to memory and knew which parts he would exaggerate, minimize, and draw to scale. He didn't need to look at him again; trusting years of experience put him at least a minute ahead of Dave.

"Dave's wasting time looking at Mr. Maguire," came a voice from the class.

"One minute," shouted the entire class.

Fen ignored the verbal blast and continued to outline the composition with bold strokes.

Two and three-minute announcements came and went. With plenty of time to spare, Fen finished the outline. It was time to add facial details and lines that showed movement.

"Four minutes!" came the cry, and Fen picked up the first colored pencil.

"Five minutes!"

Two more colors to add.

"Six!"

Dave proclaimed, "Finished!" as the timekeepers hollered, "Seven!"

Dave tried to speak over them as his hand made a sweeping motion on the pad. "And signed," he said.

"Too late for seven," said Green Hair. "Seven minutes for Dave and ten extra points."

Fen signed his name. "Finished and signed."

"That's a tie on the extra points," came the announcement from several in the room.

Without being asked, Dave moved his easel so the room could take in his work. Fen moved to where he could see.

With a wave of his hand, Fen motioned for the class to join him. "Come closer. Make notes of what you think he did well and where he needs improvement."

Fen had to admit, the sketch wasn't bad. He'd portrayed Fen in the uniform of a state trooper with a paintbrush in one hand and a cane in the other.

"Let's look at what grandpa did," said Dave.

Fen obliged and turned his easel and sketch toward the class. Exclamations of awe came forth. "Wow," said one student. "Look at the detail."

"And how he added depth by varying the intensity of the force he used on the colored pencils."

"I like the way he showed motion," said another.

"Is that a joint Dave's smoking? It's as big as a rolled newspaper," said a young man wearing boots and jeans. "Look at the oversized head and pink eyes. The sketch tells two stories."

Fen couldn't help but smile. "Twenty years of experience told me how Dave likes to start his day. That could be why he was so overconfident. The lesson is to take a prominent characteristic, exaggerate it, and tell a story."

A young lady who'd been quiet through the competition spoke up. "I could see Mr. Maguire's sketch from my seat at the edge of the first row. He finished his caricature at five and a half minutes and waited until Dave finished to give him more time."

Green Hair summarized the results of the competition. "Dave, you're good, but he's the real-deal."

Fen moved the easels to one side, making room as he moved another easel to the center. He retrieved a finished painting he'd brought with him, took off the cover, and placed it for all to see. It was one he'd recently completed, an oil on canvas that caught the sunshine breaking over a small lake in Central Texas. He knew it was good, and their wide-eyed admiration proved it.

"Take your seats, and I'll answer Dave's original question about how to make a good living as an artist."

The students settled in the first two rows. He had their attention and respect.

"The answer to Dave's question is amazingly simple. To make a good living as an artist, you have to be exceptional. To become exceptional, pay the price to become that way. I've been drawing all my life. I put myself through college by going to weekend fairs and doing caricatures. In college I minored in art and learned to paint with acrylics, mainly because I was too broke and impatient to wait for oils to dry."

"That's my story, too," said Dave.

Fen continued, "Police work helped me with my painting because I became a professional observer. I trained myself to look for things that other people missed. That skill bled over into my paintings."

"How long before the big money started rolling in?" asked Dave.

"About thirty years."

A collective groan came from the class.

Fen tried to give a word of encouragement. "It shouldn't take you so long with all the teaching tools at your fingertips. I tutor a young lady who's only nineteen. She's close to moving on from caricatures and is good enough to sell acrylics. If she keeps learning and doesn't give up, she'll be making six figures in another five years, give or take a year. In the meantime," he pointed to his caricature, "...she's catching up with me fast."

The quiet girl in the end seat asked, "Can we talk to you sometime this week?"

He nodded. "I plan on beginning a sketch this afternoon. Come back, and don't worry about interrupting me. I learned a long time ago how to talk to customers and draw at the same time."

"What will your next work be?"

"I was hoping it would snow, but it doesn't look like there's much chance of that."

What sounded like another challenge came from Dave. "How are you with cityscapes?"

"They're not my strong suit. What did you have in mind?"

"The world's smallest skyscraper. It's close to downtown."

Several in the class shook their heads while others put words to the suggestion. "Don't pay attention to him. There are better things to paint than that stupid building."

Fen considered the suggestion and gave his head a nod. "I've heard the story behind the building. It could be fun, and shouldn't take me long to take pictures and do a rough sketch. If nothing else, it'll be a good novelty item."

He took a deep breath and said, "An important thing to keep in mind is sales and marketing. There are thousands of ways to make money as an artist. Don't be afraid to try something unique, but paint what people want to buy."

"I sell gobs of pencil sketches of the waterfalls," said Green Hair. "Doing them in pencil hides the ugly color of the water."

Fen considered the deception he'd experienced when he saw the cascading water. He thought of Regina and how she'd hoodwinked so many into investing in her scheme. A pattern was developing. The world's smallest skyscraper intrigued him. Another grand deception? It wouldn't surprise him.

Chapter Twelve

Fen backed his truck into two parking spots as far away from the other vehicles as he could get. He was concerned not only about getting scratches on the new one-ton truck, but also not being able to get out. Over the years, the width of six-wheeled pickup trucks had increased while the parking lot striping narrowed. His habit was to park as far away from the entrance of businesses as possible and take up two spaces. The extra steps saved his truck from dents and dings.

Lou arrived as he pulled chilled hands from his pockets and waited for her in the restaurant's vestibule. She entered as a gust of winter's breath spun hair into her face. "Darn wind." It took both hands to pull the disheveled locks behind her ears. "Do you know what I like about cold wind?"

"Nothing?"

"Exactly. Not one blessed thing."

"Let's get seated and warm our hands on a mug of coffee."

"Hot tea in a mug will do for me."

The hostess seated them in a booth and gave an assurance that the server would be with them momentarily.

"Enough about the weather," said Fen. "How was your morning? Productive, I hope."

Lou reached into her purse for reading glasses. "I finished working my way through a big chunk of newspaper articles written about Regina. They painted a word picture of her rise to fame and acceptance. This afternoon, I'll start on the articles dealing with the scam she pulled."

"Are you reading in chronological order?"

"There's overlap, but that's what I'm trying to do. It's like reliving the crime in very slow motion."

"Any surprises so far?"

"Amazed is a better word, and it's reinforced my unhealthy distrust of people. I'm not sure I've ever seen a woman who invested so much time and effort doing good things in order to steal. That's not counting how long it must have taken her to plan it."

The server arrived and took drink orders. Fen broke tradition and ordered hot chocolate.

"Change my order to hot chocolate, too," said Lou. "It's been ages since I had hot chocolate, and this is certainly the weather for it."

A group wearing the logo of a car dealership on their jackets came in. Boisterous but not obnoxious, they moved to the far end of the room. Fen waited until they were well past before he continued. "What does your afternoon look like?"

"I'm starting on the articles Charley wrote about the crime. I'll try to review months of stories in one afternoon, but it's doubtful I'll finish today. It's not the reading, it's cross-referencing and taking notes that takes so long."

Fen nodded to keep her talking.

"The last third of the assignment you gave me is to digest all the articles Charley wrote about the victims."

Fen tilted his head. "Won't some of that information be in the second group of articles?"

"I have legal pads at the ready. My first notes deal with Regina weaseling her way into the hearts and minds of the locals. The second legal pad is for the crime, along with information on the victims, such as their name, address, and interesting background info. I'll also record the amount of investments lost, useful quotes, and long-term consequences."

The server returned with mugs of deep brown liquid with a fluffy marshmallow bobbing. Lou ordered a Philly cheesesteak sandwich while Fen selected the lunch special of meatloaf and two sides. He chose mashed potatoes with gravy and fried okra as the teammates to the main course.

The talk switched to Bailey and Thelma. He reported Thelma had checked in with him as he was sketching a building downtown. The first signs of recuperation from J.W. were showing, but Bailey was still down and out. Thelma and Libby were soldiering through without complaint.

A pensive look caused Lou's eyelids to narrow. "I hope you realize Thelma's going to demand that Bailey go home with her as soon as she can travel."

Fen puffed out his cheeks and let the air seep out. "There's no doubt that's her plan, and she won't get an argument out of me. I guess we'll see how interested Bailey is in J.W."

"What's your guess?"

Fen took a sip of hot chocolate to delay his answer. "I'm no expert on the minds of nineteen-year-old women. If it had been a simple cold, I'd say Bailey would insist on staying. Day after day of vomiting and diarrhea may be enough for Bailey to want to get home to her own bed. The deciding factor will be Thelma. If she demands that Bailey go with her, she'll stay. If Thelma gives her a choice, she'll go home."

"Reverse psychology?"

"With Bailey, I think it has more to do with age than wisdom. Both are stubborn as unbroken mules, but Thelma has the advantage of being older, wiser, and less impulsive. My money's on her tricking Bailey into thinking going home didn't come from Thelma or me."

"You're probably right. Romance comes to a screeching halt when you spend that much time in the bathroom. There's nothing like being alone in your own bed while you recover."

Lou took a full drink of her hot chocolate and changed the subject. "What have you accomplished today?"

"Nothing concerning the case. I won a competition in class drawing a caricature and watched the students study for a final exam. Then, I went to the old downtown area and sketched the smallest four-story building I've ever seen." He re-thought the last part of his statement. "It's the smallest that wasn't a doll-house or a LEGO building."

Lou continued to hold the mug as if it were a butane-powered hand warmer. "What's the entire story concerning that building?"

Of course, the reporter would want the story. He resigned himself to drinking cool chocolate later and set his mug down. In went a full breath and out came the facts as he remembered them.

"On the corner of 7th and LaSalle, near the old train depot, sits the Newby-McMahon building. It looks like a stepchild that returned from school to find his parents had moved and not told him. The architecture is late-neoclassical, which means it's drab and boring. Imagine a shoebox. It's made of brick the same color as the Wichita River—muddy reddish-brown. Tilt the shoebox long side up and you get the idea."

Their food arrived, which left Fen with a decision. He could tuck into the meal or finish his story while both his drink and his meal cooled.

Lou had no pity on him. "You talk. I'll eat."

The food smelled of home cooking and he wanted to abandon the story, but the tale seemed to beg him to tell it. Why not? It was a story worth telling.

"My source is Wikipedia." He organized his thoughts and ran a lap with the facts, legends, and myths surrounding the building.

"Railroad expansion was rampant as the 1800s steamed into the next century. Wichita Falls was one of the water stops, which led to growth.

"Things changed when they struck oil in nearby Burke-Burnett. The boom was on. Land agents came with lease agreements and royalty contracts ready to sign. The town added twenty thousand souls to pull the black gold from the earth. Railroad barons and land speculators smelled money to be made."

Lou had torn into her Philly cheesesteak. She chewed and responded only with grunts and groans.

"In 1906, Augustus Newby, one such railroad man, needed office space, so he built an office building across the street from one of the town's hotels. The single-story Newby Building could accommodate seven desks. J.D. McMahon, a land agent and engineer out of Philadelphia, occupied one desk. Remember that name.

"In 1909, Mr. Newby completed his days on earth. That was the same year McMahon began construction on an annex to the Newby Building. The completed structure would become the Newby-McMahon Building. It wouldn't be a modest structure but a four-story building. McMahon advertised it to be the grandest, most imposing structure ever to look out over the ever-expanding town of Wichita Falls.

"Investors flocked to the project. They gladly forked over two hundred thousand dollars in order to not miss out on the can't-lose investment. In today's money, that's pushing about three and a half million."

Lou swallowed. "How long until you get to the punchline?"

"I'll cut to the chase. Mr. McMahon built the four-story building like he promised, but on one-twelfth scale. All the legal documents and drawings used inches instead of feet. He never spelled out the measurements, and no one caught on what he'd done until it was too late."

He knew this was Lou's type of humor, and she didn't disappoint. Her hands came together in a loud clap, and her eyes danced with mischief. "How tall is the building?"

"Forty-eight feet tall. It should have been four hundred and eighty feet. Like I said, he used inches instead of feet."

"And the other dimensions?"

"Ten feet by eighteen. It's simple math: divide what you expect the specifications to be by twelve."

"Did they arrest him, hang him, or shoot him on the spot?"

"None of the above, but the investors claimed fraud and tried to get their money back. It went to trial, and McMahon won. He built a building according to the specifications on the drawings."

To his surprise, the meal was still warm. Between bites he asked Lou if she wanted additional details.

Lou's mouth was full, so she motioned with her head that she didn't. She pushed her plate away and reached for her glass of water. "Good story. How much truth was in it?"

He shrugged and stabbed three small bites of breaded okra with his fork. "I'd guess about ninety percent. The building's still there even though fire almost destroyed it and a chunk of a wall blew down in a windstorm. The story's good enough that they rebuilt the wall, and people keep restoring it."

Fen went back to his food while Lou asked her next question. It occurred to him that eating with an investigative reporter was a prescription for cold meals. She had a knack for peppering him with questions. She could also pack away her own meal with the speed of a ravenous teenager.

"What are you doing this afternoon?"

"Going back to the college. I have an idea for a work that I'll slap together to help me solve the case. You know how I love to paint and think at the same time. It will be a single canvas, but I'm envisioning two scenes and a portrait on the same canvas."

"That's different. What are the scenes?"

Fen put down his fork. "They all deal with deception in one form or another. First, there's the name of the city, and it's glaring lack of a natural waterfall. At the time of its founding in 1876, there was a very meager waterfall. Thus, the name Wichita Falls. Ten years later, a flood wiped it out. The only falls today is the one the city made."

Lou wrinkled her nose. "That's not a huge deception if there used to be a waterfall."

"Not huge, but tell that to all the tourists who stop expecting to see a waterfall in the river and not beside it."

He moved on quickly, knowing she enjoyed debating almost as much as Thelma did. Come to think about it, so did Bailey.

"Then there's J.D. McMahon. One third of the painting will show the world's smallest skyscraper."

Lou didn't argue about that being a whopper of a deception.

"Finally, I'll include a portrait of Regina."

He looked down at his plate and pushed it away. The gravy had congealed into a sticky glob. "By the way, I need photos of her. Can you get me some?"

"No problem. I've seen so many photos her face is etched in my memory."

"How would you describe her?"

Lou had to gather her thoughts. "She's tall for a woman. Very feminine in a conservative way with her dress and makeup. Always wore a scarf, and never a hair out of place. Average build with not much on top, but nice definition to her legs. She has something of a Roman nose with good bone structure. Her bearing is always confident, and she has a brilliant smile."

"Good description, but get me more than one photo if you can, preferably from different angles."

Lou stood. "Time for me to get back to the salt mine. Enjoy your painting."

The server came by to clear the table. "Didn't you like the meatloaf?"

"It was good, but I didn't have room for it and the pie you're going to bring me. I'll have another hot chocolate while you're at it. It seems mine got cold before I could finish it."

The pie and hot chocolate gave Fen a chance to digest the meal and the conversation. Lost in thought, the ringing of his phone brought him back from a place where deception reigned.

"Hello, Margaret. How's the detective business today?"

"Not great. Grimes and his new partner hauled Cleo Clayton in for questioning. I know how Jay works. He'll try to sweat a confession out of her. They handcuffed her, which was probably enough to flip her out. Any advice?"

"The former banker?"

"The former banker who's on strong antidepressants and God knows what else."

Fen was usually pretty good at thinking on his feet, but an immediate answer eluded him. He blamed it on the sugar rush from the pie, hot chocolate, and marshmallow.

"I'm at a restaurant. Let me pay the bill and call you back from my truck."

Chapter Thirteen

The diesel engine clattered to life. Fen took off his Stetson and placed it on the passenger's seat as a shiver raced through his body. The north wind had cut through his coat and jeans like they were thin as the scraps of paper skipping across the restaurant's parking lot. He arranged his thoughts and told his phone to call Margaret.

He wanted to give her sage advice, but because he was an outsider, it would require finesse. What he wanted to tell her was to go directly to the chief and have him intervene, but that would put Margaret in a dicey situation. Detectives had their own ways of extracting information and confessions from suspects. Supervisors gave them a good amount of discretion in how they obtained information that led to arrests. Different methods work with different people.

Fen believed Grimes used a one-size-fits-all method that included threats, intimidation, and deception. He based this on Margaret's use of the word interrogation instead of interview.

Margaret answered on the first ring. She spoke in hushed tones. "Yeah."

"Where are you?"

"In the ladies' room. They've been going at her for ten minutes."

Fen pictured the scene in his mind. "Are they still playing nice?"

"For now, but it won't last long. Patience isn't one of Jay's strong points. He starts off with about fifteen minutes of smiles and background questions. You know, simple stuff and all buddy-buddy. He'll then lower the boom and tell her they have some sort of proof that she killed Charley, and she'd do herself a favor by telling her side. Of course, she'll deny she killed him and he'll give her a look to let her know he thinks she's lying."

"Guilty until proven innocent," said Fen. "Does he then tell her he'll check her claim against the evidence he already has?"

"It doesn't surprise me you know the game. This is when he takes a break for at least half an hour. He'll come back and tell her that not only did he verify the original evidence, but a lab report came in that proves her guilt. He'll come down hard and won't let up until she breaks. She'll either have a complete mental breakdown, or he'll get a confession."

Fen puffed out his cheeks and blew out a puff of air. His thoughts went to his farm manager, Sam. Years ago, the same thing had happened to him. Circumstantial evidence combined with lazy cops and a district attorney who wanted a quick conviction. They railroaded Sam into prison for a murder he didn't commit. It took years for Fen to undo the injustice.

He knew what to do, and the first thing was to make sure Margaret didn't overreact. "Listen carefully, Margaret. Don't do anything. In fact, get out of the office as quick as you can. Grimes isn't after Cleo. He's setting you up."

"No way. He's a pain in the neck, but he'd never do that."

Fen put steel in his words. "You're wrong. Something

happens to cops like Grimes when they get toward the end of their career. They want things to be the way they were when they were young. He can't stand that you're smarter than him and that you'll someday be sheriff or the chief of police."

"I can't allow him to coerce a false confession out of Cleo."

"I'll take care of him. You stay out of it. We've embarrassed him in front of his junior partner already. Losing face at this stage of his career is a pill he can't swallow. Believe me, he's using Cleo to set you up." He paused. "If you don't believe me, call your father."

"You said you'll handle it. What will you do?"

"First, I'll ask Hope to call her attorney. He'll have Cleo home before dark. That will put a quick end to the Grimes's plot. He may accuse you of making the phone call, but that's something you can deny without lying. It might even backfire on him."

"And the second thing?"

"That's a more long-term fix to your problem. It's best I don't tell you about it."

He could tell Margaret was teetering on what to do. She needed to take action on something that wouldn't jeopardize her career. He gave her the name of the restaurant. "Come get me. Let's take a road trip to see Lisa Stuart."

"Why?"

"To get you out of town, and I did a lousy job when I interviewed her. She knows a lot more about her ex-husband than she told me. Also, we're stalled out on finding Regina. If you don't want to drive that far, we can try to interview Mason."

"I don't think there's anything we can ask Mason about his brother that Dad didn't ask."

"Perhaps not. That's why I want your perspective on Lisa." He didn't allow her time to make an excuse. "Call your father on the way to pick me up. I'll take care of getting Cleo away from Grimes."

"I'm not leaving the office until I talk to Dad. If he agrees with you, we'll go. If not, I'm going to the chief."

The call clicked off. He told his phone to call Hope and prayed she'd answer. She did, and he told her he needed help.

"What kind of help?"

"A rescue mission. Detective Grimes has Cleo in an interrogation room. I believe he's trying to clear a murder case by using a shortcut."

"That man needs to retire before he ends up costing the taxpayers. I take it you need an attorney to protect Cleo?"

"If it's not too much trouble."

"More of a pleasure than trouble."

Fen's next call went to Lou. "Are you reading articles?"

"Not yet."

"I have an assignment for you that you'll like."

He imagined Lou picking up a pencil and taking notes. "You have my undivided attention. Please tell me it's not doing research."

"Some, but not much."

Lou loved details, so he gave her the long version of the story. He imagined Lou's blood pressure rising with each sentence. By the time he finished, Lou was champing at the bit to boil Detective Grimes in newspaper ink.

"Can I call out Grimes by name?"

"Let's try being subtle first. I doubt your editor would go for that kind of story."

"I hate it when you're right. Ever since Charley offended so many people, the newspaper is hesitant to print much of anything that shows the town and its citizens in a negative light."

"Go to the editor and tell him you have an idea for an

article about qualified immunity for police officers. It's what protects them from prosecution. Make it general, but work the angle that the law is slowly shifting away from giving police free rein to lie and deceive during interrogations. Be sure to use the word interrogations and not interviews."

"I get it. Make the article about old-school cops like Grimes, but don't use his name."

"That's the idea. Be sure you mention cases where cities have had to shell out big bucks for abuses. Monetary settlements always scare supervisors and elected officials."

He could almost hear the gears in Lou's brain locking into place. This was her kind of story, and she'd latch onto it like a mechanic's vice.

"Any questions?" asked Fen.

"Can you get Cleo out before she crumbles?"

"Hope's attorney should arrive at the police station soon."

"Photos are what I need. I'll also try for an interview, but not too hard. If Grimes tries something like this again, I'll have plenty of ammunition to use in the next article."

"Let's hope it doesn't come to that, but it's a good idea to have another story ready to go."

Lou wasted no time ending the call, which was typical for her when she had an assignment.

A few minutes later, Margaret's unmarked SUV pulled into the parking lot. He knew Hap would want to protect his daughter from what could have been a needless mistake. Right or wrong, junior detectives don't tell senior detectives how to interview. He'd seen more than one career derailed by zeal.

The north wind hit him as soon as he slammed the door to his truck. The Stetson almost cartwheeled across the parking lot before he anchored it with his left hand. He entered the all-too-familiar interior of a police car. The sights, sounds, and smells were like returning to a high school reunion; it was familiar but part of the past.

His first words were, "That wind is vicious. Is it always so windy up here near the border?"

"If you lose your hat, don't worry. Someone else's will blow to you before long."

Fen chuckled. He'd heard the joke before from a West Texas sheriff. It was still a good one, and it told him Margaret had her head screwed on straight again. "What did your father say?"

She waited until they were on a city street to answer. "He told me to listen to you and do what you say." Her top lip quirked. "He also said I'd better watch my back. I wasn't sure if he was talking about Grimes or you."

"Both, if you're smart. There are sometimes fine lines between being shrewd, sneaky, and sinister. I try to stick with the first two."

"How would you judge what you're doing to my former partner?"

"Shrewd up to now, but I have a plan for sneaky if he doesn't back off."

He wanted to let the distasteful business with Detective Grimes play out on its own. One way to do that was to switch topics. "How well do you know Lisa?"

"Not great, but my father devoted long hours investigating her." She cut her eyes to look at him. "That reminds me. I need to update her file."

"Not a bad idea. Can you do that from home?"

"Sure." She tapped a rhythm on the steering wheel, applied the brakes and turned into the parking lot of a convenience store. Once stopped, she put the car in park and turned to face him. "This trip to see Lisa is a waste of time. You wanted me out of town so I wouldn't do something stupid, like I was planning."

She'd caught him, but he didn't want to give up the ruse without a fight. "What are you talking about? Lisa is still a suspect."

"She lives almost two hours away and there's nothing in the files to show she ever spoke to Regina. She'd moved to Fort Worth and divorced Charley before Regina arrived in Wichita Falls. You said yourself that she received a windfall of money from an inheritance." Giving her head a nod, she said, "It was in the neighborhood of half a million dollars. No wonder she lives by a golf course."

Fen held up his hands. "I surrender. Take me back to my truck."

She wagged her index finger at him. "You weren't kidding when you said you could be sneaky."

"Not sneaky enough. You busted me fair and square."

She pulled a tight U-turn in the parking lot and headed for the street. "What are you doing the rest of the day?"

"Going back to the university to paint and think. How about you?"

"I'll go somewhere besides the police station and establish an alibi in case Jay accuses me of something."

"You can get online at the university and work from there."

"It's been a while since I darkened the library's doorstep. It'll be like old times."

Margaret dropped him off at his truck. He remembered to hold a hand on top of his hat. His thoughts turned to Bailey and whether she was showing signs of improvement. He'd better call Thelma.

After cranking the engine, he placed the call. As was her habit, Thelma got in the first words. "It's 'bout time you checked in. Stop at the store and pick up some cough syrup. Honey and whiskey aren't cutting it."

"How much whiskey are you giving her?"

"It's not for Bailey." A racking cough seized the house-keeper and self-appointed nurse. The storm had to pass before she said, "There's somethin' in the wind that don't like me, and I'm not fond of it, either."

"I'll get something for the cough and pick up some antihistamine pills as well."

"Don't make a special trip."

"I was going to paint at the university this afternoon. I can do that in my room."

"You don't have to hole up by yourself. J.W.'s vertical again and taking in food. He wants to watch you paint. You can use his studio upstairs."

"How's Bailey?"

"Better. A day behind him in recovering. You'd best come up with something to occupy her mind besides that handsome young man upstairs."

Chapter Fourteen

The day was turning out to be a series of distractions. The first came when Detective Grimes detained Cleo Clayton. She was perhaps the most vulnerable of all the people victimized by Regina, Charley, and the board of directors at the bank she worked for.

He'd had to come up with an idea to keep Cleo away from Grimes and, at the same time, make sure Margaret didn't fire a torpedo into her career.

He also thought about Lou. Instead of getting him photos of Regina Cox and doing research on Regina and Charley, she was at the police station taking photos. When she finished that task, she'd write a story about qualified immunity. Another waste of time with no guarantee that Detective Grimes would take the hint to stop his strong-arm tactics.

Fen watched a young tree bend in the wind as he parked his truck in the driveway of Hope's home. "Not one sketch done yet." He really wanted to paint a winter scene of freshly fallen snow on the vast plains of North Texas while he was here. Instead of a carpet of white, he'd seen nothing but wind-blown dust. As for his habit of painting to help him think, he hadn't completed a sketch, let alone put paint on canvas.

"That's something I can control," he said with determination in his words. "I'm starting on my sketch of the falls and the tiny skyscraper this afternoon. The portrait of Regina goes on as soon as Lou gets the photos to me."

The camper shell of his truck held everything he needed. He opened it and retrieved a large sketch pad, a framed canvas, and his box of artist's pencils. He strode toward the house with confidence that he'd salvage the day.

The wind ripped the canvas from his hand when he was halfway to the back door. Not a good start to the second half of his day.

Fen made his way into the mansion and dropped the load in his bedroom. His next stop was Bailey's room. She bid him to enter at his knock. "How's the patient?"

Bailey was sitting up in bed with several pillows supporting her back. "Not great, but better." Her voice sounded weak, but it was good to see a little color in her cheeks.

"Any fever?"

"None so far today. Knock on wood." She didn't find wood, or even look for any. "My stomach finally stopped doing cartwheels. I should be able to help you with the investigation by tomorrow."

He had to think fast. They had an unwritten agreement that she could help with investigations in a limited capacity. She'd proven herself to be a great asset in obtaining information from children, teens, and young adults. Unfortunately, all the suspects in this case were older. Nothing came to him. Time to delay until he found something she could do.

"Where's Thelma?"

"Probably in the kitchen. That's where she and Libby hang

out. From what little I picked up when I wasn't in the bathroom, they won't be buying each other Christmas presents."

Fen turned toward the door. "I'll be back."

Bailey may have been one of the most street-wise people he'd ever met. She could spot conflict and deception like it was a pimple on her nose while getting ready for a date. She gave him a sideways glance that spoke louder than the words that followed. "Don't bother coming back if you don't have something useful for me to do."

She followed up her pointed statement with, "You need to send Thelma home. She has her mind set on taking me home with her. I'm staying here with you until we finish this case."

This was what he'd feared and what he didn't want to deal with: two immovable objects. In addition, he sensed Thelma and Libby were about to collide in a battle of words and wills. Throw in strong-willed Bailey for good measure; not good.

"I'll handle Thelma. You get well."

Before going to the kitchen, Fen remembered the cough syrup he'd purchased. He returned to the truck, retrieved the medicine, and chased his wind-snatched hat across the driveway. What else could go wrong?

Once in the kitchen, he wished the thought hadn't crossed his mind. Thelma sat at the kitchen table with a plastic squirt bottle of honey and a half-empty bottle of whiskey in front of her. She looked up and blurted, "It's 'bout time you came home."

A deep cough followed her words. She filled a shot glass full of whiskey, then honey filled a tablespoon. In a two-step operation, the honey went in her mouth then she chased it down with the whiskey. The shiver started at her waist and didn't end until her head shook. "Best cure ever for a silly old cough." She looked up through rheumy eyes. "Want some?"

"No, thanks. I brought the cough syrup you wanted."

"Don't need it now." Another deep cough followed her proclamation.

He stepped to the stove, where Libby stood watching something boil in a pot. He whispered, "Was the bottle full when she started?"

"She broke the seal and hasn't stopped." A string of expletives in Spanish followed.

Fen rubbed his face with the palms of his hands. "I'd better get Thelma to bed and take over caring for Bailey."

Libby turned to face him with a butcher knife in hand. "She stays out of my kitchen, or you'll investigate another murder."

That answered the question of how Libby and Thelma got along. He'd been afraid they were too much alike and now had confirmation. No matter how big the home or kitchen was, there wasn't room for both of them. Bailey was right. Thelma needed to go home.

"I understand," said Fen. "Bailey's on the mend, so there's no reason for Thelma to stay here."

Thelma shouted with slurred words, "What're you two talkin' 'bout?"

Fen didn't make a practice of lying, but this occasion called for stretching the truth. He moved to the breakfast table. "I was asking her about J.W. Libby says he's doing much better."

"Bailey is, too, thanks to me. You'd be in a bucket of pickles if I hadn't come."

Fen wasn't about to say or do anything to contradict her. He needed to get her out of the kitchen before Libby's knife slipped. "Let's go check on Bailey."

If Thelma hadn't consumed half a bottle of whiskey, she wouldn't have fallen for his ploy. As it was, she made it to her feet and charted a course to the wing of the house that held their bedrooms.

After a few bounces off the walls, she made it into Bailey's room. Thelma claimed her palm was more accurate than any thermometer ever made. She swayed back and forth as placed a hand on Bailey's forehead and announced, "Ninety-eight point seven."

Bailey looked past Thelma to Fen with her eyebrows raised. He answered her unasked question by using his fist and extended thumb to signal someone taking a slug of booze.

Fen knew the next challenge was to get Thelma to sleep off her home remedy and to think it was her idea. Bailey came to the rescue. "I feel so much better. I'd like to get out of bed and see something other than my bathroom. What's your room like, Thelma?"

"Same size as this 'un, but it's got different paintings on the wall, and the bedspread ain't the same."

Thelma turned to Fen, swaying back and forth. "No use in you staying here. Me and Bailey are gonna' look at my room." She poked his chest. "No men allowed."

He wanted to give Bailey a hug. Instead, he handed her the plastic bag containing the bottles of cough syrup. One was a daytime formula, and the other came with caution not to drive or operate machinery. He thought either would be enough to put Thelma down as long as she took a full dose.

Fen excused himself and went to his room. With the door shut, he moved into the bathroom for added privacy and placed a call to Sam, his ranch foreman, who was also Thelma's husband.

As usual, Sam answered with a grunt. Unlike Thelma, who could rattle on about anything and everything, Sam used words as if someone had only allocated him a few and they had to last the rest of his life.

"Thelma needs to come home tomorrow. She developed a cough and used honey and whiskey to cure it."

"How much?"

"Half a bottle."

"Too much. Put her in bed."

"Bailey's doing that now. Can you call her tomorrow morning and tell her to come home?"

"Is Bailey better?"

"Much improved—no fever, no cough, and she wants to help with my investigation."

"Thelma leaves tomorrow."

"Thanks, Sam." The call clicked off. Fen knew if there was anything of significance to report at his home and farm, Sam would have told him. He also knew Sam was the only person in the world who could get Thelma to leave without Bailey. Their relationship remained one of the great mysteries of life. Sam spent most nights living outside while Thelma had a bungalow behind Fen's garage. To any visitor, it appeared as if they lived completely different lives. Not so. Their relationship might be different, but it was stable.

With the assurance that Thelma would leave without Bailey the next day, he set up his easel and sketch pad. A knock on his door sounded.

"Mission accomplished," said Bailey, as she walked in wearing a robe over flannel pajamas.

"Any trouble?"

"She balked at taking a dose of cough syrup until I told her it contained honey and whiskey. I'm not sure how much she was supposed to take, but the bottle is down a third."

"That's at least a triple dose. I guess if it doesn't kill her, it'll cure that cough."

Bailey looked at the sketch pad. "What's the project?"

Fen took his darkest pencil and drew three lines on the page. "I'm dividing the page into thirds. The waterfall in the park will be one scene." He took out his phone and pulled up the photos he'd taken of the waterfall.

"That water is yucky."

"The rain before we arrived got the river to flowing and stirred up the red dirt bottom."

"What's the second sketch going to be?"

"Keep scrolling through the photos until you find the world's smallest skyscraper."

Bailey let out a laugh when she saw the building. "That's the craziest thing I've ever seen." She then asked, "What's the final open space for?"

"I'm reserving that for a portrait of Regina Cox."

Bailey studied the three blank areas on the giant page. "I get it. Three things that all speak of deception. You're going to paint them to help you think."

He appreciated Bailey's ability to put together the three scenes and know his plan. She was learning the same skill he'd developed over the years of losing himself so deep in a painting that it seemed to talk to him. He'd solved several tough cases by that method. It was in the deep state of flow that he put together clues and answers came to him.

"Can I do the portrait?"

"No." The answer shot out before he could corral it.

"Why not? I'll need to stay around the house for at least another day. Thelma told me you're working with Detective Sibley to find that Regina woman. You still have to go to the college in the mornings. With all that going on, the least I can do is help you by painting a portrait you'll never sell."

The answer came to him like it blew in on the wind. "I have another project for you."

She looked skeptical, so he kept talking. "Call Lou and tell her to bring photos of the murder victim. Get to work on sketching his individual facial features."

Bailey gave him a sideways glance. "Is this busy work?"

"Not at all. Someone killed him, and I don't believe the locals will discover who."

Bailey wobbled. He moved to her side. "Let's get you back in bed."

She didn't argue, so he wrapped an arm around her and guided her back to her room. Straightening her bed covers, Fen asked, "Have you had anything to eat today?"

"Thelma tried to get me to eat some oatmeal and toast this morning, but I wasn't ready for it."

"What about now?"

She shook her head. "I'll call Lou for the pictures then take a nap. Food almost sounds good again, but not yet."

Bailey placed her robe on the foot of the bed and slipped under the covers. "I promise I'll be ready to sketch before dark."

"Do the eyes, nose, and mouth first. Each on a separate page. You can use a small sketch pad and pencils."

Instead of putting up a fight, she pulled the covers up to her throat. "That's good. I can stay in bed and sketch. Tell Libby I'll be ready to try her cure-all soup when I wake up." Her eyelids drooped. "It'll be our secret that I ate Libby's cure."

Fen walked into the hallway and found Hope eavesdropping outside Bailey's open door. She motioned for him to follow her with a tilt of her head.

He closed the door of Bailey's room and went on offense, "I arranged for Thelma to leave tomorrow morning."

"That's probably for the best, but I need to talk to you about something else. Detective Grimes is on his way to the hospital with a broken arm."

Chapter Fifteen

F en followed Hope into a room he hadn't been in yet. It was intimate, almost like a private retreat. Its diminutive size, lack of electronics, and worn, but still serviceable, leather furniture gave it a cozy feel. There were no windows, only two chairs set at an angle, a matching couch, and a scarred coffee table. The leather was shiny in spots from years of wear, and the coffee table looked like it had experienced its share of boots, some with spurs attached.

Hope closed the door behind them. "This is my thinking room. It's where I come when I need to be alone."

The room had the smell of an old saddle. The only personal item was a photo of Hope's late husband. Fen pointed at the photo. "My office serves the same function. I go to it every morning and talk to my late wife."

"We have more in common than I thought," said Hope. "Most people don't understand. They think I should move on. I can't, and I'm at peace with it."

The lump in his throat kept him from doing anything but

nodding in agreement. He pushed down his emotions and waited for Hope to retrieve a tissue and dry her eyes.

She cleared her throat and spoke with renewed vigor. "Detective Grimes tried to push his way into Mason Cleg's home. He was foolish enough to have his arm in the doorway when Mason slammed the door. He then threw himself against it and broke Grimes's arm. Mason weighs upwards of three hundred pounds."

"Did Grimes have a warrant?"

Hope answered with a single shake of her head. "That's not his style."

"Was Mason arrested?"

"Other officers took him into custody. They were booking him into jail when the chief heard the circumstances and released him. He'll put Grimes on administrative leave if he returns to work. This may well be the end of Jay's career in law enforcement."

Fen put the pieces together and saw into the future. He needed confirmation. "Who will take over the murder investigation?"

"The best detective we have is Margaret. Since she's already consulting with two former sheriffs on a case that intersects with the murder, it's like getting three top cops for the price of one."

"Does Margaret know yet?"

"The chief will tell her sometime today." She gave him a brief smile. "You don't look surprised."

"It was only a matter of time for Detective Grimes. You're also right about the two cases being linked. Now that Margaret has access to all the forensic information, we can make some headway."

A question raised Hope's eyebrows and furrowed her brow.

"Are you telling me Grimes didn't allow Margaret to see information that could have helped you?"

"No need to dwell on that. She'll have access to everything today."

Hope pursed her lips. "Combine that file with Hap's and Margaret's, and you'll have all the information."

Fen didn't mention the information and conclusions Lou would come up with by scouring past issues of the local newspaper. He also didn't tell her about his plan to allow the three-part painting to speak to him. She was a practical woman who probably wouldn't appreciate something that far outside the norm.

His mind shifted into high gear as he added motives for murder to the mix. A knock sounded on the door, interrupting his thoughts. Hope shouted a command to the person knocking to enter.

Libby opened the door enough to say, "Telephone, Señora."

"Sorry about the interruption," said Hope as she rose and left the room. She closed the door behind her.

Fen found himself alone. He realized if he didn't call Lou, she'd make him pay for not giving her a news scoop. He fished his phone from the pocket of his vest and told it to call her.

She answered with a quick, "I'm busy. Make it snappy."

"Did you know Detective Grimes is sporting a new cast on his arm?"

"Details."

"He tried to strong-arm his way into Mason Cleg's home and left with a broken arm. He forgot to get a search or arrest warrant. They took Mason downtown but didn't keep him. Grimes is out and Margaret is running the murder investigation and the search for Regina."

"What's your source?"

"Off the record, it's Hope."

She huffed out an expletive. Lou's three least favorite words were, 'Off the record.'

"This changes everything," said Lou. "Are you sure Mason isn't locked up?"

"Not according to Hope."

"I'll track him down and get the story."

A click ended the call. Tact went by the wayside when Lou had a hot story on the line.

Fen had bought himself a favor by notifying Lou of a breaking story. He knew she'd find Mason and get a front-page column. Building up favors never hurt.

With that task taken care of, he had time to think, so he focused on Hope. She was a mover and a shaker in the city and county, but she was more than that. It was like she was the matriarch of the county and a regal queen bee at that. How much power did she wield, and was it benevolent?

Years of dealing with criminals and politicians taught him to suspect people in positions of power and influence. Power could be used and it could be abused. He wondered about Hope, and his concerns bubbled under the surface.

He even allowed his mind to consider Hope as a suspect. Could she be involved in the murder of Charley? How did she wield such power and influence? Was it possible that she had him killed?

He answered his own question. Charley had caused untold damage to many residents of Wichita County. If Hope was the queen of the county, then she'd failed. Part of a queen's job was to protect her subjects. Punishment awaited the offenders. There was no doubt she wanted Regina found so she could pay for her misdeeds. Was it too much to imagine Hope taking her anger out on Charley?

Fen's imagination was running at full speed. If Hope had been involved in Charley's murder, the best way for her to remain above suspicion was to keep Grimes in charge of the murder investigation. As things now stood, a dream team of investigators would work together to solve both cases.

He folded his hands together, closed his eyes, and wondered how cunning Hope was. Could she pull off the perfect crime? If so, the investigation would die a slow, quiet death.

Lost in thought, he heard someone cough. It was a fake cough that signaled someone approaching to talk. Looking up, he saw J.W. standing at the door that he'd silently opened.

Fen waved the young man in. "Your mom received a phone call."

J.W. approached the sofa. "Nothing new about that. Mom stays busy. How's Bailey?"

"She's better, but tired. How about you?"

The leather creaked when J.W. flopped down. He was a lean young man before the illness. Now, he looked malnourished. "Tons better than I was. I'll be in class tomorrow."

"Just in time for finals. Are you ready?"

"I'll do all right. I was exempt from all but two." He looked around the room, but there was precious little to look at. "Any progress on finding Regina?"

Fen dodged the question by asking, "How old were you when she disappeared?"

He looked up at the ceiling. "I'm pretty sure I was in my first year of high school. It was big news and seemed to go on forever. Mom took it hard, especially when the newspaper articles kept blaming people for being so gullible."

Fen was on the verge of asking another question when J.W. started talking. "I asked Mom why Charley returned to town when so many people hated him here. She said she didn't know."

"That's the best question I've heard all day. Since I haven't been working on the murder case, I don't have an answer for you."

"Don't you have an idea? I know Mom tries not to show it, but she's obsessed with finding Regina. Finding who killed Charley could be a part of that."

The declaration confirmed what Fen suspected. J.W. was concerned that his mother had thought too long and hard about both cases. He also knew children sometimes go to great lengths to protect their parents, especially their mothers. He wondered if J.W. had taken Charley out of the picture to take pressure off his mother. Another suspect? Perhaps.

The young man rose like he was a marionette, and the puppet master had lifted his bones with strings. Now upright, he asked, "How long before Bailey can leave her room?"

It was good to hear a question that he could answer with certainty. "Tomorrow. I'm not saying it will be before you go to class, but she'll be up and dressed by the time you get home. I've given her an assignment."

"She's lucky to have you teaching her."

"I'm the lucky one."

Hope returned, shaking her head. "I'm sorry, but there's an emergency with several of the Christmas floats. The wind is plucking the FFA's giant chicken, the Baptists's bible lost its entire book of Psalms, and the bank's Window of Opportunity is closed for business. I told them to pay attention to the weather forecast and wait to put on anything that could blow away. We even held a special training session for the proper way to secure paper flowers on chicken wire."

"Let them figure it out on their own, Mom. Something like this happens every year. You can't keep trying to rescue everyone."

Fen couldn't help but notice the concern in J.W.'s voice for his mother. He wondered again if that concern could lead the sensitive young man to eliminate a major cause of her distress.

Hope ran a hand down her son's cheek and waved to Fen over her shoulder as she headed toward the door. "One of these days, I won't be around to pick up the pieces."

With Hope gone, Fen followed J.W. out of her sanctuary and closed the door. The mood seemed unnecessarily somber. He placed a hand on J.W.'s shoulder. "I understand you have a studio upstairs. Do you mind if I take a look at it?"

J.W.'s angst melted away as a wide smile returned. "Mine won't compare to yours, but you're welcome to see it. I'm sort of stuck on getting the ears right on a portrait I'm working on."

"The good thing about ears is, they don't have to look exactly alike. Most have differences. I need to make a quick phone call, and then I'll be up to take a look."

He retreated to his bedroom and placed a call to Margaret. It went to voice mail and he spoke after the prompt ended, "Margaret, this is Fen. Make an appointment for us to speak with Mason tomorrow. He'll need some time to calm down after the day he's had. I'll be available any time after eleven."

The remainder of the afternoon was finally available for him to sketch and start painting. Only one thing left to do: Go upstairs and get a better read on J.W. After all, he was at the hotel when Charley died. A case could be made that he had motive, opportunity, and means.

Chapter Sixteen

The last student to finish the final exam dropped the test booklet and answer sheet into separate baskets. He was a droopy-eyed young man who had nodded off during the test.

Fen asked, "How'd you do on the exam?"

The answer came with a huff of exasperation. "This class was supposed to be an easy A. Who cares about a bunch of dead European artists? All the paintings and sculptures look the same to me—old and boring." He looked away, and then, just as quickly, brought his gaze back. "Oh well, I'll squeak out a C."

"What method did you use to guess?"

A confident smile came to the young man. "If it's multiple choice, I use logic and the process of elimination. There's usually a clue given in the question."

The phrase *process of elimination* caught Fen's attention. He wasn't expecting the bleary-eyed young man to have planned a strategy for taking tests. "Give me an example."

"Several of the questions started with, 'Who was the Italian artist who painted such-and-such?' I looked for names that ended with an I or an O. That eliminated artists like Van Gogh, Renoir, and a bunch of others. I came to enough classes to get a general idea of who were the big guns and figured their names would show up most often. If it came down to a name I recognized and one I didn't, I'd go with the most famous. After all, this is an intro class."

"What about the true-false questions?"

"My chances are fifty-fifty on those before I look at the test. The odds improve if I read the question carefully. I look for absolutes and guess false if I see one."

"Absolutes?"

The student spoke with certainty, "Any question that has the word all, never, must, or anything like that is probably false. You also have to remember that the university professors and instructors want the grades to reflect a bell curve. Their business is to keep students coming back until they extract as much money as they can from us. If you learn how to take tests, you can get a degree and not have to study much."

Fen concluded the student was equal parts cynical, practical, a realist, and lazy. He wished the young man well and meditated on the conversation for several minutes. The time spent pondering made him realize he needed to eliminate suspects from the murder investigation.

Margaret entered the classroom, causing him to refocus. She'd pulled her hair back into a ponytail, a good choice on another cold and blustery day. "It looks like I waited long enough. Are you ready to go?"

"I'll need to drop off these final exams for grading, but we'll do that on the way out. Let's take a few minutes and get a game plan before we visit Mason."

Margaret looked around the classroom. "Here?"

Fen looked at the desks in neat rows. "Would you rather go somewhere and get coffee?"

"Not really. I was so wound up after what happened yesterday that I couldn't sleep last night. I've been up for hours drinking coffee. Any more, and I'll shake like the few remaining leaves on the trees."

Fen motioned for Margaret to sit in the chair behind the instructor's desk. He pulled a student desk from the front row and placed it to the side of the instructor's desk. This showed Margaret she was in charge of the case, and he was there to help.

Once they were both seated, Fen asked, "Did Grimes make much progress?"

"He and the forensic team did a good job searching Charley's hotel room. The lab had no trouble concluding the cause of death. It was poison that came in a bottle of whiskey. He questioned the hotel staff, and no one remembers anyone delivering a bottle to his room or him picking up a delivery at the desk. The hotel's video footage revealed nothing helpful."

Fen spoke as possibilities crossed his mind. "That helps a little, but not much. He could have brought the bottle with him."

"If he did, we'll need to expand the search of suspects to people he knew in Fort Worth."

"It's also possible someone met him in the hotel's parking lot and gave it to him there. If so, he knew them well enough to recognize them and accept the gift. They could have stayed with him until they were sure he was dead and wiped the place clean. It's also possible Grimes or his new partner missed something as they reviewed hours of hotel video."

Margaret didn't seem surprised by his logic. "The fire alarm makes me believe your theory about someone being in the room with him when he died. I picture them together, waiting for the popcorn to pop and having a private happy hour. If so, either Charley or the visitor made a mistake when setting the timer on the microwave. It overheated, caught fire, and caused the evacuation."

Fen appreciated her quick mind. "I know the hotel has cameras covering the front desk and some of the other areas, but not all. It was a cold, rainy night, and people covered their heads with hats, hoodies, and scarves. Do you know how thorough Jay was in studying the videos?"

Her ponytail bobbed up and down. "It's hard to tell, but he made a list of suspects. You, Bailey, and J.W. were at the top."

"Doesn't surprise me. How in depth were his background checks?"

"The one he did on you was thorough, but he expressed frustration with Bailey's."

"How so?"

"Heavy underlines and question marks on his notes. He scratched a message to himself to get juvenile records. That didn't work out, so he made calls to people who know cops in Houston."

Fen looked past Margaret. "That fits for a guy like Jay. It didn't take long for Bailey to make an enemy out of him. Even if he knew she had nothing to do with the murder, he'd want to make life miserable for her."

"Next, he focused on J.W., but only because he changed clothes in Bailey's room. He didn't dig deep on him and not at all on his mother."

"Untouchables," said Fen in an off-hand remark. He tilted his head. "What about you and your dad? Did you make the list?"

"Our names were there, but he drew a line through them."

Margaret moved on. "Cleo and Mason had stars by their names and a couple of pages each on background."

"Did he run fresh bank statements on everyone you've mentioned so far?"

"Only on Cleo and Mason. There was a note for him to start a list of everyone Charley had bad-mouthed in his articles. It was in the section with bank records, so I assumed he wanted to put that off until after interviewing Cleo and Mason."

"What about Charley's ex-wife?"

"Nothing recent, but he had the records my father ran on her."

"Better safe than sorry. When you get time, run fresh financial statements on Lisa." He blew out a huff of air. "If I remember right, there could be up to fifty local people who invested and lost money. Getting bank statements and interviewing that many people will require long hours of tedious work."

Fen realized what he'd done. "Sorry. You're running this investigation, not me."

She dismissed his statement with a wave of her hand. "If there's one thing I've learned by being the daughter of a sheriff, it's appreciating his hard-earned wisdom. He's still two or three steps ahead of me in catching bad guys. You and Dad think alike. He wants everyone to meet tonight at our place."

Fen let out a chuckle. "I was going to recommend that same thing."

The pending meeting with Mason rose to the front of Fen's thoughts. "Did you have any trouble talking Mason into meeting with us?"

"He hung up on me. Dad called him back and smoothed his ruffled feathers. I didn't know it, but Mason dodged a DWI way back in high school. That was years before his brother carpet-bombed everyone he could with newspaper articles."

Fen understood without asking. He and Margaret were cashing in on a favor Hap had kept in his back pocket for years. That didn't mean they'd get much useful information out of Mason, but at least it got them in the door.

Margaret cast her gaze to him. "There's something else that happened yesterday, and you're not going to like it."

Fen raised his eyebrows when she paused.

"Larry Fry, the cop who took my place, deployed a tazer after Mason broke Jay's arm."

Fen rolled his eyes. "No wonder Mason hung up on you. I wouldn't be very talkative, either."

"Mason didn't get shocked. It was Rex, his dog."

Fen groaned. "Did he kill the dog?"

"Larry's lucky Rex is a big German shepherd." She paused a little too long.

"What else?" asked Fen.

"The first officers responding to the call are good buddies of Jay and Larry. Jay told them to take the long way through town. When they arrived to book Mason into jail, he'd somehow slipped when getting into the back seat of the SUV."

She put air quotes around the word slipped.

"What's the damage?" asked Fen.

"They broke Mason's nose."

"Let me guess. Their body cameras malfunctioned."

She confirmed his words with a nod. "This may not be a productive interview."

"Only one way to find out," said Fen. "After the interview, I plan on coming back here and spending the rest of the day painting."

The ringing of Fen's phone put a temporary hold on the conversation. Bailey's voice sounded crisp and clear. "Where's your truck?"

"Here at the university. What do you need?"

"A blank canvas. I also need to stop by the newspaper and pick up some photos from Lou."

Fen huffed in frustration. "I'm tied up with an interview for the next hour with Margaret. I'd tell you to use Thelma's truck, but she went home this morning."

Bailey groaned. "She didn't wake me to tell me she was leaving."

"Sometimes having a lousy memory is a blessing. This is one of those times."

He could almost see Bailey nodding. "What happens in Wichita Falls stays here?"

"Exactly."

Bailey moved on quickly, "J.W. and I are going stir-crazy. I have the spare keys to your truck and Lou is expecting us. All I needed to know was where I could get a blank canvas."

J.W.'s voice sounded distant. "Don't worry about it, Bailey. I have plenty."

"Before you go, remember to spend extra time drawing Charley's eyes, nose, and mouth."

Another thought came to his mind. "Make it a competition between you and J.W. Give me charcoal sketches of only the face without ears, hair, or neck."

"I thought you wanted a full portrait in acrylic."

"Hold off on that until you and J.W. do the charcoal sketches."

"Is that all?"

"One more thing. When you get photos from Lou of Charley, tell her I need a head shot of Regina. Leave it in my truck or take it back to Hope and J.W.'s. I'll sketch her when I get a chance."

"J.W.'s waiting on me. Got to go."

Fen looked to his left. Margaret had a twitching smile at the corners of her mouth.

"What?" asked Fen.

"You're a lucky man to have a daughter like her." She held up a hand to stop the denial of Bailey being his daughter. Instead, Margaret changed the subject. "Let's see if we can get some useful information from Mason."

Chapter Seventeen

The mid-morning traffic was light, so there was no delay in the trip from the university to Mason's home. It was a modest frame home in a rather down-in-the-heels neighborhood. Fen guessed it to be a Vietnam-era three-bedroom dwelling with a rusting, metal carport. The one-car garage was long ago converted into a room by someone who cut corners with materials and labor. An inflatable Santa lay flat on the grass waiting on its motor to fill it with life-giving air.

Margaret had exercised an economy of words since leaving the university. She'd gripped the steering wheel too tight, and worry lines made spider web lines from her eyes. He waited for her to speak.

"How do you want to handle the interview?"

Fen had asked himself this same question on the trip across town. "It's important that we put Mason at ease. That may take a while, and I'm a stranger to him. He must respect your father, or he wouldn't have agreed to the interview. You start by focusing on your father with small talk." He looked again at the home. "What kind of work does Mason do?"

"He works in the lumber department of the local Home Depot."

"Talk about lumber and hardware if you run out of things to talk about. Also, be sure you ask about his dog. You'll probably get an earful, but it'll be a lot less awkward if you get that and his injuries out in the open. Don't allow him to dwell on it too long, or he'll shut down and this will be a waste of time."

"Acknowledge, but don't emphasize. I understand. What will you be doing?"

He'd come up with a plan but wanted it to play out without her knowing what to expect. "I'm going to make a friend out of an enemy."

This had the intended effect on her of having to trust him. Her skepticism, however, won the first round. "You'll need to be a good magician to pull that rabbit out of your hat. Mason isn't the friendliest guy you've ever met, even when things are going his way. His wife gave him the boot after Charley wrote a scathing article about them and how stupid they were for cashing in his retirement savings to invest in Regina's scheme."

Vicious barks came from the far side of the door even before Margaret knocked. Fen reconsidered the wisdom of entering the home. German shepherds have an inbred desire to protect persons and property. Unless controlled, things could get ugly.

Margaret took a step back when the dog hurled itself against the solid wood barrier. "Let's hope Rex isn't seeking revenge for yesterday."

"Whatever happens, don't go for your pistol. Keep your hands where Rex can see them."

A deep voice hollered from inside. "Shut up, Rex!"

The command had little effect until the voice advanced on the door and repeated the command two more times.

"Is that you, Margaret?"

"It's me and a former sheriff who's helping me. His name is Fen Maguire."

"Your dad told me about him. Let me get a leash on Rex. Don't come in until I tell you to."

The two waited in the cold, which was better than being a chew toy for a dog with a score to settle with anyone who had the smell of a police vehicle on them.

"Come in," came the command.

Margaret led the way, keeping her hands at her side. Fen followed with a valise tucked under his arm and hands free with palms where Rex could see them.

Mason had a firm grip on a thick leather leash that was hooked into a metal choke collar encircling the neck of the black and blond guard dog. Rex lunged toward him, but Mason expected it and had planted his feet firm enough to hold him back. The choke collar did its job and Rex soon realized the futility of trying to attack.

Mason took a seat in an aging recliner with gray duct tape on one arm. He commanded Rex to sit by him and took up the slack on the leash by wrapping it around a beefy hand. He then pointed to a couch. Words weren't necessary for Margaret and Fen to understand that was where they were to sit.

Mason's nose had a white strip of tape covering the bridge. Yellow and purple radiated out under both eyes.

Margaret lifted her chin and spoke with clear, short sentences. "Thanks for seeing us. Like I said, this is Fen Maguire. He's a former highway patrol officer and was a sheriff for ten years. He's also a well-known artist who's helping at the university."

No response came from the scowling man.

Margaret kept talking. "Fen's helping Dad and me try to find Regina Cox."

"Why?" asked Mason.

Fen answered, "We're hoping she hasn't spent all the money she stole, and we can get some of it back to the victims."

The snort told Fen that Mason wasn't holding out much hope for recouping his losses.

Margaret cleared her throat and scooted forward on the couch. "What happened yesterday wasn't right, and those responsible will answer for what they did to you and Rex."

Fen reached into his valise and took out a sketch pad along with three pencils. Rex sat on his back legs, ready to spring, with ears erect, never shifting his gaze from the two intruders. As Margaret continued, he captured the image of the German shepherd at full alert.

"Daddy wanted me to tell you he's sick about what happened to you."

"It ain't his fault, but I appreciate his words all the same. He's always been more than fair with me." Mason seemed to look back into years gone by. "Did you know he could have put me in jail when I was a teenager? I was plenty drunk driving home when he pulled me over. He told me that was my one and only chance to straighten up."

"Dad never mentioned it to me until last night."

"Don't surprise me none. He called my parents and told them to come get me and my truck. My Pa did more to me than any judge would have. As it was, I had to walk everywhere I wanted to go for two months. Took me almost that long before I could sit down without it hurting, and it was in January and February."

"How's work going for you?" asked Margaret.

"Not bad. It's steady, so I can't complain." He took in a deep breath. "I know you didn't come here to shoot the breeze. What can I do for you?"

Fen kept drawing and allowed Margaret to carry the conversation. "As of yesterday, I'm in charge of the investigation into your brother's death. Do you know why he came back to town?"

Fen glanced up in time to see Mason stiffen at the mention of his brother.

"I don't know and don't care. Charley stopped being my brother when he wrote that article about me and Sue Ann."

"Do you blame him for Sue Ann leaving you?"

Mason ran a calloused hand up and down his face that looked like it hadn't seen a razor in four days. "I can't say he was totally to blame, but it was a big log on the stack of little sticks. Sue Ann still hasn't remarried, so there may be hope. Money had a lot to do with us splitting the sheets and still does. I pick up extra shifts whenever I can."

"You're still in close contact with Sue Ann?"

"Ain't no getting around it until the kids are eighteen."

Mason cast his gaze to Fen and then back to Margaret. "Is there really a chance of getting money back if you find Regina?"

Fen kept drawing as Margaret answered. "I don't want to get your hopes up, but it's possible we could recover some of the money. The first step is to find her and get her back into the country."

Fen broke his silence, "That's assuming she's not already here. It seems she planned everything out with incredible precision, which leads me to believe she could be living in the States under an alias. Assuming a new identity is difficult but far from impossible."

Margaret took up where he left off. She explained how someone could hide in plain sight if they lived modestly and had meticulously planned taking on a unique identity.

Fen put the finishing strokes on the sketch, tore off the sheet from the pad, and handed it to Margaret. She looked at it and showed her admiration with eyes opened wide. "This is amazing."

"Give it to Mason and see what he thinks."

Mason rose, and so did Rex. They came forward, and Margaret held the sketch in front of Rex, who looked at it and tilted his head. A confused look crossed the dog's face. His tail wagged.

Fen took over. "I could do better if I had more time. Rex's eyes are very expressive."

Rex cast his gaze at Fen, and his tail wagged faster.

"He likes it," said Mason.

Fen rose and came from behind the coffee table. He held out his hand for Rex to smell.

The dog not only sniffed it, but gave it a lick.

"He never does that," said Mason with surprise in his words. "You've made a friend for life. Can I keep this?"

"That's why I drew it. Merry Christmas."

"I'll get it framed and give it to Sue Ann and the kids for Christmas."

Fen took his seat on the couch, letting his gaze take in the room that lacked a feminine touch. The only nod to Christmas was four monogrammed stockings. This was working out better than Fen had hoped, but he needed to get more information about several people who used to be in Mason's life. He made a quick mental list, moved to the edge of the couch, and gave Rex a scratch behind his ear.

"It's safe to take him off the leash," said Fen. "I'll do another sketch of him while I'm asking you some questions. Can you get him to lie down with his paws in front of him and his head up? I'll spend more time on this one."

A wide smile came to Mason. "If it's not too much to ask, could you do two more? One for each of the kids. You're saving me a bunch of money I don't have for Christmas presents."

"No problem."

Mason snapped his finger and pointed to a spot in front of his recliner. "Lay down." Rex obeyed with head up and paws in front of him, looking at Fen with expectant eyes.

"Perfect," said Fen as he took his sketch pad and began to outline Rex's form and face. "Tell us what Charley was like as a child."

Chapter Eighteen

F en's question about what Charley was like as a child brought a quick reaction from Mason. "My brother was a pain in the neck. He was older than me by several years. Book smart, which was a good thing because he was always sick with allergies. Reading and writing stupid stories was how he spent his early years."

As was his habit when interviewing, Fen nodded at regular intervals to keep the flow of words coming. He asked, "How did his illness affect you?"

"If you've ever heard of a momma's boy, that was Charley. Never got in trouble and always made the honor roll. He might have known how to write a story for the school newspaper, but he couldn't change a flat tire or screw in a light bulb." With a growl to his voice, he said, "He was sneaky and held grudges like you wouldn't believe."

"Can you give us an example?" asked Margaret.

Mason gave his head a firm nod. "I saved to go to a really cool summer camp the year I was going into the fifth grade. Mom said I could go if I earned the money to pay my way. I mowed lawns and made enough, but when it came time to pay, my money was gone. Charley told Mom I'd spent it on video games and I was trying to get her to pay for it. She believed him over me. It wasn't long before Charley mysteriously came up with enough money to buy a printer for his computer."

Margaret shook her head. "That's a lousy thing to do to a brother."

"Like I said, he was sneaky and smart. He had telling stories down to an art, and I can't remember him ever getting caught. There's no telling how much he stole in high school. The teachers all thought he hung the moon because of his good grades."

Fen asked, "Did he cheat on tests?"

"Didn't need to. Like I said, he was scary smart." Mason hesitated. "There is one thing you need to know about Charley. When he pulled the stunt that kept me from going to summer camp, I got my revenge."

A malevolent crinkle of a smile visited Mason's face. "Charley would sneak out late at night to see his girlfriend. I knew he was doing it, but Mom never suspected he'd do something like that. One night I waited in the yard behind a tree with a rock the size of a softball. It was about one-thirty in the morning when he came home. The rock caught him square in the back of the head and he went down like I'd shot him."

"How long was he out?" asked Margaret.

Mason shrugged. "A while. I took the rock, threw it as far as I could over the back fence and went back to our room. He stumbled into bed around first light. He confronted me about it a few days later. I told him there were plenty more rocks where that one came from. He never stole from me again."

"Do you think that's why Charley wrote such a scathing article about you?"

Mason spoke through clenched teeth, "I have little doubt

that Charley enjoyed writing that article, but he didn't limit his hatred to only me. I think that smack on the head scrambled his brain. He was smart and sneaky before, but he became mean after that."

The interview was going better than Fen expected, but he wanted more. "Did you stay in touch with Charley when he went off to college?"

"Only through Mom. She was forever telling me about how good his grades were. He'd earned a full academic scholarship and set his sights on being a big-city reporter. He wanted to go into television but didn't have what it takes. His voice was high, and I thought he looked like a wet cat on the demo tapes he sent home to Mom."

Mason kept talking. "It came as a surprise when Charley married Lisa. She was several years younger than him and was good looking." He gave his head a shake. "I've got to hand it to Charley. He always attracted nice-looking girls. There's something to be said about being smart. It's almost as if they can smell out someone who's going to be a good provider."

Margaret jumped in, "If I remember right, Charley was in graduate school when Lisa got pregnant."

"Mom was so disappointed. Her perfect son had finally made a mistake. They married, then he dropped out of graduate school and got on at the local newspaper. Losing the baby kicked Charley harder than I thought it would. He was always good to Lisa, but he coped with the loss by turning into a workaholic. I guess it eventually took its toll on their marriage, and Lisa called it quits."

Rex opened his mouth wide as he yawned with a curled tongue. The sound of the top sheet tearing off from the pad signaled the completion of the second sketch. Fen signed it and handed it to Margaret.

"Oh, yeah. This is even better than the first." She held it up for Rex and Mason to see. Rex's tail waved back and forth as Mason nodded his approval.

"Does Rex have a favorite toy?" asked Fen. "I want to show him being playful."

Mason responded without delay. "Rex. Get Snoopy."

Toenails fought to gain traction on the hardwood floor. The shepherd skidded around a corner and disappeared down a hallway. He returned in a matter of seconds with a stuffed likeness of the beloved beagle in his mouth. The angle was perfect for a side view with his head facing Fen.

"You're a natural model, Rex," said Fen. "I wish humans could pose like you do."

He started on the third sketch. "Tell us more about your former sister-in-law."

Mason's eyebrows rose and then fell. "Not much more to tell. I only saw Lisa on special occasions. She worked in a pharmacy, always dressed nice, and drove a new car. Charley didn't care what he drove, but Lisa would trade every two years for something new and sporty."

Fen thought about the woman who was now living in a golf community. She'd impressed him as a woman who took extra care to look her best and drive newer cars. Nothing wrong with that, as long as the inheritance held out.

He nodded for Margaret to take over as he focused on Rex. Her question was one he'd planned on asking. "What people come to mind when you think about who may have killed your brother?" She followed up the question with a qualifier. "We realize your answer will be pure speculation, but we value your perspective."

He scratched the whiskers on his chin. "Since we've been talking about Lisa, I'd say the chances of her killing Charley are next to zero."

"Why's that?"

"No motive. According to Mom, their marriage was more like a high school romance that sort of fizzled out. He went his way, and she went hers. No kids, no fight over property. She was gone long before Regina came to town and Charley hit the big time with his reporting."

"Who else?"

"This may be a long shot, but Hope Ellison might have seen to it that Charley caused no more trouble. She's a powerful woman who never got over losing her husband."

Mason looked into the kitchen for no apparent reason. "I wonder what Charley was doing in town."

Fen quipped, "We do, too. We were hoping you could tell us."

"Mom might know, but I don't have a clue."

Margaret and Fen traded glances. It was a signal for Margaret to follow up with Mason's mother.

"Anyone else?" asked Margaret.

"There's a bunch to choose from. Charley rubbed a lot of salt into open wounds."

Margaret didn't mince words with her next question. "Did you kill your brother?"

Instead of being offended, Mason simply shook his head. "If you'd have asked me that two years ago, I'd have kicked you out of this house, because I was planning on killing him then. But after a while of not seeing him, my hard feelings faded. I'm not saying I'll ever forgive Charley for all he did to me through the years, but he's gone, and that wipes the slate clean. I'll take Mom to the funeral, but I won't grieve."

Fen asked, "Any other ideas of who might have killed Charley?"

"I like to watch cop shows. They always say to start with those closest to the victim and work your way out. The problem with Charley is, he had no one he was close to that I know of.

Even Mom lost faith in him after he wrote those articles about how stupid people were to invest in Regina."

Once again, Fen traded glances with Margaret. They seemed to ask each other if it were possible a mother would poison her son.

Fen put the question aside and went back to his sketch. Mason directed his question to Margaret. "Who does your father think killed Charley?"

"Dad and I are hoping the answer to that question will somehow lead us to Regina. Right now, everything's still as muddy as the Wichita River."

Mason had one more question. "How long before I don't have to look over my shoulder for Grimes's cop buddies to pull me over?"

This was a question Fen had known would come. No matter how wrong Grimes had been by trying to force his way into Mason's home without a warrant, a detective had sustained a broken arm. The brotherhood of the badge was strong.

Margaret took a stab at an answer. "The chief came down hard on Detective Grimes and Larry Fry. He's also suspended the cops that roughed you up."

"I'm tempted to get an attorney and sue their socks off."

"That's your prerogative," said Margaret.

Fen expounded on her response to give a more complete picture. "Any time you sue, you place yourself in an adversarial position. It's you and your financial resources against those of the city."

"If you were in my shoes, what would you do?"

"Nothing for at least a week or two. That will give you time to cool off."

"And then?"

"I'd like to think I'd let it go."

Mason shook his head. "I'm not leaning that way."

"Then you'll have an uphill battle. Start by deciding what you're willing to settle for and how much money you can pour into fighting the system."

"I think I'm due a six-figure settlement."

"You may get it, but you won't get it all. Your lawyer fees and court costs will add up."

"Tell me how to start."

Fen took in a full breath. "Start by collecting information. The more you can do on your own, the less you'll have to pay an attorney or private investigator. Submit freedom of information requests for body camera and dash cam footage from every officer involved. That includes recordings from the jail. Collect medical records for any treatment you've received and any follow-up visits. Hire an attorney to write a letter that threatens a lawsuit if you don't get fair compensation."

"Won't that make the city council mad?"

"They're already mad, but not at you. They're mad at the cops who conducted an illegal entry into your home, caused you injuries, and violated a slew of departmental policies."

"It sounds like you think I should sue them."

Fen firmed up his words. "Lawsuits are for fools. Only the attorneys win. Don't get greedy, and be ready to compromise. From what I know about the chief, he's already planning an extensive retraining program for all officers."

Margaret interrupted, "Fen's right. The email came out this morning. All officers are to attend mandatory training on the use of force and when and how to apply for warrants."

Fen finished the subject by saying, "The cops overreacted. Make sure you don't do the same. Don't expect to get a huge settlement, and realize your attorney fees and medical costs will get most of it."

He tore off the last drawing, stood, and handed it to Mason.

This put a smile back on Mason's face.

Margaret also stood, as did Rex. She gave her new four-legged friend a pat on the head and looked up at Mason, who'd also made it to his feet. "Thanks for your time. You've been very helpful."

He looked at the last sketch. "I feel like I should pay you for these."

Fen waved off the comment. It was well worth it for all the information. "I hope your family enjoys them."

Rex saw them to the door and received parting pets and ear rubs. They waited until they were in Margaret's SUV before she asked, "What next?"

"Focus on bank accounts and find out what you can from Mason's mom. I'm going back to the university to paint the rest of the day."

"What about tonight?"

"I'll call Lou. You talk to your dad, and let's see if we can't make progress around your kitchen table."

Chapter Nineteen

F en wheeled into the driveway of Hap and Margaret's ranch. It had been a productive day. Bailey was on the mend, and Thelma had arrived safely back in Newton County. He'd finally had time to sketch the first two images of what would become a three-scene painting. He'd also finished his responsibility with one college class and turned in the final exam for grading. Mason had provided a wealth of information on his brother, sketches of Rex would bless two children, and hopefully a marriage could be stitched back together.

Still thinking back on the day, Fen's thoughts rested on the portrait he'd finally started. It took him almost three hours to get into the flow. It always took time to kick his mind out of gear and allow his subconscious to bring things to his remembrance. That was when the separate pieces of a case came together. He believed that with another day or two of painting, his mind would take seemingly unrelated facts and put them in order. It all depended on whether he had enough facts.

Margaret opened the door for him and bid him to enter.

The smell of Christmas spices and baking cookies met him like an old friend.

"I hope I'm not late. I see Lou's Camry. Has she been here long?"

A coy smile quirked her lips. "Lou's car was here when I arrived at five-thirty. She and Dad came back from riding horses just before dark. They've been in the kitchen trading recipes."

Fen stopped in his tracks. "Lou doesn't ride horses, and she's never expressed a love of cooking anything but strong coffee."

"She seems to enjoy baking now."

"Well, paint me white and call me a picket fence. I never thought I'd see the day when Lou would climb up on the back of a horse or open the door to an oven."

Margaret cupped her hands the way people do when they share a secret. "Dad asked me what I thought she'd like for Christmas."

"What did you tell him?"

"I said perfume, but I'd have to ask you what she likes."

"Me? How should I know? I can tell you what my wife liked, but I don't know about Lou. Probably something that smells like newspaper ink."

"A typical male answer. I'll call Bailey and ask her."

He slipped out of his coat and handed it to Margaret, who hung it in the hall closet. Wind-blown hair required he smooth it with the palms of his hands. They walked toward the sound of laughter. When he rounded the corner, Hap removed his hand from Lou's. It reminded him of a time when Sally's father caught them holding hands. They were in the ninth grade, and he still remembered the threatening stare her father gave him.

Fen pretended not to notice the smirks on both their faces.

Instead, he looked at Lou and tented his hands on his hips. "What's this I hear about you wanting a pony for Christmas?"

A pink hue rose into her neck. She stammered, which made the scene funnier. "Uh... it was fun... and cold."

"She's an excellent rider," said Hap. "No pony for her. She needs a horse at least fourteen hands high."

Lou changed the subject. "Did you finally get to paint this afternoon?"

Fen gave a nod. "I got started." He pulled out a chair on the opposite side of the table from Lou. Margaret slid into the chair next to Lou while her father sat in his usual place at the head of the table.

"How far did you get?" asked Lou.

"I finished two sketches and got the base colors on canvas."

"I'm lost," said Hap. "What are you painting?"

"It's a single canvas with three scenes," said Fen. "The first is of the waterfall in town. The second is the tiny skyscraper and the last will be a portrait of Regina. Answers to tough questions come to me when I paint."

Hap chuckled. "That's clever. Three things that show deception." He thought for a moment. "It's probably best that you don't show them to Hope. After Regina and Charley tore the county to pieces, she's touchy about anything that doesn't show the county in a positive light."

Lou gave Hap a sideways glance. She wasn't a fan of censorship in any form. She'd been let go from her job as a top reporter at a major newspaper in Dallas because she stepped on the toes of politically powerful people. Everything she wrote was true, but she experienced what can happen when you cross powerful people.

Fen spoke quickly to keep the meeting on track. "I thought we'd each give a report on any progress we've made on the case.

Margaret and I had a good chat with Mason this morning. Why don't we share about that interview first?"

Margaret began by giving praise to Fen for winning over Mason by drawing sketches of Rex.

Hap looked at him with new admiration. "Of all the ways to get on someone's good side, that beats anything I ever tried. Do you use it often?"

"Not that often, but it usually works."

Margaret stated she believed they should leave Mason on the list of suspects. She justified her decision by telling the story of young Mason hitting Charley with a large rock. He'd shown no remorse for that childhood act. Next, she noted that Jay Grimes had suffered a broken arm and Mason didn't ask how serious the injury was. Finally, he expressed no grief about his brother Charley being murdered.

Hap asked, "Did he have an alibi for the time when Charley died?"

Margaret shook her head. "Not unless Rex learns to talk. He claimed at the jail that he and his dog were home alone watching television."

Lou wasn't one to hold back on expressing her opinion. "I think Detective Grimes got what he deserved."

The crossed arms of the former sheriff of Wichita County told Fen they needed to move on quickly. Injuries to officers were a touchy subject with anyone who wore a badge.

"I agree with Margaret. Mason needs to stay on the list of suspects. Hap, who's at the top of your list?"

He took his time answering. "I have no solid proof to back up what I'm about to say, so it needs to stay in this room. Hope is a wonderful woman, but Charley made a powerful enemy out of her with the stories he wrote. I'm not saying she killed him, but it wouldn't surprise me if she knows who did.

"She's worked herself to the bone trying to rehabilitate the reputation of the city and county. I believe she's taken on more responsibility than what's healthy. Charley's murder, and even you two getting involved in trying to find Regina, must be taking a toll on her."

Lou gave her head a firm nod. "Charley's stories were so over the top, it's hard to believe the editor allowed them to be published."

"The former editor," said Hap. "Hope saw to it that he lost his job."

Lou's shoulders rolled back and her left eye twitched. Not a good sign, so Fen hurried to head off an eruption from the woman he knew was an unapologetic champion of freedom of the press. "Margaret, were you able to interview Mason and Charley's mother?"

Her head bobbed. "I talked to her this afternoon. She cried more than she talked. Between sobs, she admitted Charley disappointed her by not fighting harder for his marriage to Lisa and later with the articles he wrote. She tried to get Charley to back off on his stories, but he overreacted. They had a big falling out and all but stopped talking."

"Do you still have her on your list of suspects?"

"A mother's love is hard to break. She's at the bottom of my list. In fact, I'm getting discouraged. There are at least forty more local people who lost money to Regina's scheme. What she and Charley did is still sending ripples through the county."

"I agree," said Lou. "Look what the police did to Mason. There's no excuse for that type of retribution."

Hap countered with, "Don't you mean what Mason did to Jay? He didn't deserve a broken arm or getting suspended before the chief heard his side of the story."

"Of course, he did," said Lou. "He broke the law by trying

to force his way into Mason's house. He's lucky Mason didn't shoot him."

Fen groaned. The dam had breached. A flood of words was on their way. He thought about trying to push them back, but two strong-willed people were past the point of muzzling their mouths.

"How can you say you want a cop to get shot?" asked Hap.

"Don't twist my words. I said he was lucky he didn't get shot. Wouldn't you shoot someone trying to break into your house?"

"Jay wasn't breaking in. Mason's known him all his life. He had to have known Jay would want to talk to him about Charley. It looks to me like Mason was obstructing Jay's investigation."

"Do you really believe cops don't have to follow the same laws as everyone else?"

Margaret leaned forward. "Dad, I think—"

"Stay out of this, Margaret." Hap's tone brooked no argument.

"Let her talk," said Lou. "She's in charge of this case, not you."

"Or you," shouted Hap. He pointed to Fen. "That goes for him, too."

"Then it applies double to you," said Lou, with fire in her eyes. "No wonder they didn't reelect you as sheriff."

"At least I have a conscience. That's not a requirement for reporters." He tilted his head to look down at her. "It's a good thing the editor told you he wouldn't publish your story about Jay's broken arm."

Lou raised her chin and spoke with too much pride in her voice. "It's impossible to muzzle the truth. I sold the story to newspapers in Dallas and Fort Worth, and two television stations. Hope may own the local paper, but the free press is bigger than any one person."

Fen pushed his chair back. "I came here to help solve a murder and find a missing thief. Have any of you considered that Charley might have poisoned himself?"

He stood as the other three looked at him with mouths hinged open. Without saying another word, he walked to the front hallway, retrieved his coat, and headed to his truck. A cold north wind cut through his jeans and chilled his face. What had started as a productive day now blew into scattered pieces. He wondered how things had unraveled so quickly. At least he'd given them something new to consider, even if he didn't believe it to be true.

Chapter Twenty

By the time Fen entered Hope's home, it was almost eight o'clock. He'd taken his time driving across the county and even stopped for a hamburger. It sat heavy on his stomach. A fair amount of self-loathing had attacked him for not controlling the situation between Hap and Lou. He'd hoped opposites would attract. Not forever, but long enough for a short Christmas romance and to solve the two cases. No such luck. Their differences were too great, and the thrill had chilled. He doubted Lou would ever place her foot in another stirrup.

Thoughts of being home, watching logs burn in his fireplace, and sipping hot chocolate floated across his mind. He missed the quiet, solitary life he'd made for himself. It was one of those times when he wondered what he was doing so far from home.

The back door closed behind him and Bailey met him in the hallway. She wasn't smiling.

"What's wrong?"

"Mrs. Ellison wants to talk to you."

It wasn't the brevity of her words, but the way Bailey said

them that caused him to puff out his cheeks. The queen had summoned him.

"Where is she?"

"In the small room with old furniture."

Hope didn't rise to meet him. Instead, she motioned for him to sit on the couch. He considered defying the non-verbal regal command but wanted to give her the benefit of the doubt. He settled in with his back against the caramel-colored leather.

"What progress have you made with your investigation?"

"Investigations," said Fen as a way of countering the accusatory tone of her question.

"There's only one investigation." Her words reminded him of flint striking steel. "You agreed to help the police find Regina. From what I hear, you're no closer to finding her than the day you arrived. Furthermore, your woman reporter friend is as bad as Charley."

"You're mistaken about the singular form of investigation. The police have also asked me to assist them in finding who's responsible for Charley's death. It's possible there's a link between the two crimes."

"No. It's you who are mistaken. Your services are no longer requested by the police chief or the sheriff."

Hope had been busy. Lou's television story had struck a raw nerve. He responded to her by doing the one thing she wasn't expecting. He cut loose with a loud, inappropriate laugh.

Anger flashed in her eyes. "I can't see any humor in your friend bringing hurt and harm to this community. You and your colleagues have shown yourselves as inept and disruptive. You are no longer welcome in this county."

Fen stood. "What's funny is that you think you can run me out of *your* county. I'll stay as long as it takes to solve both cases, and there's nothing you can do to stop me. As for Lou Cooper, expect more stories from her. Enjoy the ones on television tonight and in tomorrow's Dallas and Fort Worth newspapers."

"Get out!"

"Thank you for your hospitality. I'll send you a check for room and board."

Fen eased the door shut behind him and left Hope to stew. He went to the distant wing of the home to gather his belongings.

Bailey met him with her winter coat and knit cap on. "Don't worry about packing. I put our bags in the truck."

He put a hand on her shoulder. "I'm sorry you have to leave, too."

"I'm not. J.W. has everything I could want in a man except a backbone. His mother made him tell me to pack our things. Who wants a boyfriend like that?"

"Let's get out of here."

Fen closed the door behind them. Somehow, the wind didn't feel as cold.

The truck cleared the front gate, and Bailey breathed a sigh of relief. "Are we going back to the hotel?"

Fen nodded. "Lou should be there by now. Her mini-romance ended tonight, too."

"No, it didn't. She said after you left, Hap told her he'd never considered Charley might have killed himself. You spurred a lively discussion. He apologized and said a woman who spoke her mind was one he could admire. He told her he knew she wouldn't be around long, but he wanted to spend more time with her."

"Go figure," said Fen. "People never cease to amaze me. Just when I think nothing can take me by surprise, up pops something else."

"Like a tough case to solve?"

"You read my mind. This one has me tied in knots."

Fen didn't realize how slow he was driving until a car passed him like he was a three-legged turtle. He pressed the accelerator and the truck sped up to a more reasonable speed. "Did Lou say when she was coming back to the hotel?"

Bailey snickered. "She said she'll join us for breakfast, but not before seven. I'm not waiting up for her."

"Good. I want you and her to go to Fort Worth tomorrow. You may need to drive."

He looked over in time to see Bailey wiggle her eyebrows. "I knew Hope couldn't scare you off the investigations. What do you have planned for us?"

"We need to find out all we can about Charley."

Bailey turned in her seat. "We have reservations for three more nights at the hotel. I called after J.W. told me his mom was giving us the boot."

"Good thinking. I doubt Hope would try to shut us out of every hotel in town, but you never know."

"What did you do to make her so mad?"

"I don't believe I did anything." Fen collected his thoughts and smiled. "I looked in my crystal ball recently. I saw you becoming a very successful artist. Fame and fortune came to you suddenly."

Bailey's blond hair shook from side to side. "Have you been drinking?"

"Nope."

"Smoking the wrong type of cigarettes?"

"I'm stone-cold sober. Let me finish." He took in a full breath. "Life has a way of blessing us and kicking us in the teeth. What do you see when you look at Hope?"

"She's too rich, too busy, and too bossy."

Fen tilted his head and gave a sideways nod. "Good summation, but there's a lot more to her than money and wanting to control. The kick of a horse took her husband from her. She's trying to fill the void he left."

"With what?"

"Good works, and protecting the county by making it a better place to live."

"She can't. People will always do bad things."

"What happens to us when we really want something but can't have it?"

Bailey took a couple of seconds before answering. "I get frustrated."

"And then?"

"I say things I regret."

They'd come to a stop sign with no traffic coming. He didn't proceed through the intersection. "I did the same thing tonight. I should have kept my mouth shut, but I told Hope we weren't giving up on the investigation and there was nothing she could do about it."

"Good for you."

"It was the right thing to do but not the right thing to say. I spoke in anger. If I'd kept my mouth shut, I could have left without offending her."

"You're too nice." Bailey brought her gaze full to him. "What's the point you're trying to make?"

Fen swiveled in his seat to return her gaze. "You have a deep sense of right and wrong. Someday, you'll have a lot of money. Maybe not as much as Hope, but more than enough. With wealth comes power, or at least the illusion of power. You'll face situations you'll want to control. Use Hope Ellison as an example of what it looks like to go too far."

Bailey pointed to the road. "You can go. I heard you."

They made it to the hotel without incident and unloaded their suitcases. After checking in, they headed to their rooms, this time on the third floor. While walking to the elevator, he spotted Carmine, the maintenance worker.

"Carmine," said Fen. "We meet again."

A blank stare morphed into a look of recognition. "Yeah. I remember you."

Fen extended a hand of friendship. "I've always wondered what type of things a maintenance man has to fix at night."

"You name it. If it doesn't break on its own, someone will give it a hand. Most of the time, it's simple stuff like television remotes that need batteries or light bulbs. You wouldn't believe how many people steal bulbs."

"Some people," said Bailey.

Carmine's gaze shifted to Bailey. "Yeah. Some people is right. Can't trust 'em."

Fen looked for a reason to keep the conversation going, but nothing came to mind. Bailey came to his rescue. "You sound like you're from Chicago. Am I right?"

This earned a smile. "Yeah. I'm hoping the Cubbies make a run next year."

Fen joined in. "You're not a White Sox fan?"

Carmine grimaced. "It's Cubs or nothin', and don't get me started on the Yankees."

"How long have you been working here?" asked Fen.

"Five years." A shadow of anger crossed his face. "Five long years."

"What brought you to Wichita Falls?"

"The promise of a quick buck."

"Ah," said Bailey. "Did it have anything to do with a real estate investment?"

"You're too young to know 'bout that." Suspicion came to his stare.

Fen held up a hand. "We know a woman reporter who's

investigating the old real estate swindle. She's also staying here in the hotel."

"If she's anything like the guy who got himself killed, I hope she moves on." He took a better look at Bailey. "Now I recognize you. That guy and you were in the pool when the alarms went off. You gave the cops a hard time, and they almost cuffed you. I gave you and that young man blankets."

"And a towel," said Bailey.

Fen needed to get back on track. "You told me you had a college degree."

"Yeah. Sociology. I shouldn't have wasted my time and money." He drew a line with his hand across his face. "Up to my ears in debt when I heard about the can't-miss investment opportunity. I begged and borrowed enough to come here and plop down what was required. The next thing I knew, I was stuck here, broke, and bummed out. It's taken me all this time to dig myself out."

"Are you close to getting your head above water?"

"Another year, and all I'll owe is student loans."

Carmine's radio paged him to go to room 409 to look at a slow-running bathtub drain.

"Got to go. It's always something."

Fen and Bailey waited long enough for the elevator door to close behind Carmine. They entered a second elevator and didn't speak until the stainless-steel door slid shut. Bailey asked, "Was he on your suspect list?"

"He is now."

Fen wondered how many others they could add to the short list of suspects. Instead of eliminating people, the list grew larger.

Not wanting to overtax his brain at this late hour, he asked something he knew Bailey could answer. "Did you get a good start on your painting of Charley?"

"Not really. I did what you told me and sketched his facial features. I was going to start on the painting tomorrow, but Lou and I are going to Fort Worth."

The elevator door opened, and they stepped out onto the third floor. "Lou can handle what I have in mind by herself. You can come with me to the university and work on your painting. I'll join you in the studio after I finish with the class taking their final exam."

"A full day of painting?"

"That's the plan."

"I wish it was something more interesting than noses and ears."

"It will be good practice for you. Do another round of sketches of the individual parts and try to achieve flow as fast as you can."

Chapter Twenty-One

The smell of bacon and coffee activated Fen's taste buds as soon as he entered the hotel restaurant. The night's rest was dreamless, uninterrupted slumber, the kind that left him rejuvenated and eager to begin the day. He hadn't realized until last night how poorly he'd slept under Hope's roof. It was as if her anxiety permeated every square foot of the oversized home.

He ordered coffee and thought about the level of peace he experienced in his home back in Newton County. What made her home so different from his four-thousand acres and more-than-adequate home? He answered his own question and gave his former wife, Sally, all the credit. She'd accepted her impending death and coached Fen on how she expected him to behave after she was gone. Her peace remained.

Hope processed her husband's death differently. The self-appointed matriarch of Wichita County immersed herself in civic activities. She tried to replace her husband with all manner of good works. It was as if she was trying to make him live through her.

Bailey's arrival at the table put an end to his thoughts of Hope. "Did you sleep well?" He turned over her coffee cup to signal the server to give Bailey her morning jolt of stimulant.

"I slept great. Much better than at the Ellison's. I thought it was because I was so sick, but that place has a weird vibe."

They each finished their first cup of coffee in comfortable silence. Whereas Fen habitually rose before first light, no matter the season, Bailey and early mornings rarely got along very well. A seven o'clock breakfast meeting stretched her civility to its limit. For her to admit to a great night's sleep bordered on miraculous.

Lou was the next to arrive. A scrunchy held her hair in place at the back of her neck. A leaning beret covered the top of her hair and part of one side. Dark, half-moon circles slept under eyes without makeup. She tried to say, "Good morning," but the first word came out as a squeak, leaving only "morning."

Bailey looked like she would goad Lou. Instead, she took the first sip from her second cup of coffee. Fen knew better and turned over Lou's cup. She'd made it downstairs on time. How late she'd stayed up last night with Hap was none of his business.

The booth had room for one more. Margaret took the last spot directly across from Lou. She carried with her a valise that she opened. "I made a copy of all Daddy's files and my research on Regina." She sat next to him and leaned at an angle to bring herself closer. "I thought I could get you the file on Charley's murder, but the chief told me that one couldn't leave the office. By the way, none of you are to come to the office."

Fen made sure his words didn't carry beyond their booth, even though no one sat nearby. "How much trouble did Hope cause for us?"

"It's not us anymore. It's me with a new partner. You,

Bailey, and especially Lou, aren't welcome in the city. I'm not here talking to you if anyone asks."

"What a crock," said Bailey.

"I second that comment," said Lou.

Fen held up a hand to silence them. "We need to make this quick. There's no need to cause Margaret grief."

"This will be the last time I can meet any of you in public."

Lou had sparks coming from her otherwise tired-looking eyes. "If Hope thinks she can push me around, she can take her queen's scepter and stick it."

"Hush," snapped Fen with enough steel in his voice to cause Lou to recoil. He shifted his gaze back to Margaret. "What can we expect?"

"Harassment in the city. Nothing serious, but Jay's buddies have a green light to find reasons to pull all three of you over, especially Lou. The chief received a phone call from you-know-who. Jay's punishment wasn't supposed to go public. Hope kept it out of the local paper, but not the ones in Dallas and Fort Worth. That might not have been so bad if the television station hadn't carried the story."

Margaret cast her gaze to Lou. "You made a powerful enemy out of Hope."

Lou flipped the words away as if they were a fly trying to land on her coffee cup. "Not the first time."

"I'm hoping the hotel doesn't kick you out today." Margaret turned to Bailey. "You and Fen won't have to leave until after the Christmas parade because Fen's helping out at the college and not charging them."

He received the information with a nod. "I'll communicate only through your father unless it's something urgent. You'd better get out of here."

Margaret took a drink of her coffee. "A rich, bossy woman might make me do things differently than I normally would, but she won't stop me from using every resource available to solve the cases."

"Glad to hear it. You'll make a top-notch chief someday. In the meantime, I suggest we concentrate on finances. See what you can find concerning Charley and whomever you count as top suspects."

Fen held up an index finger. "One more thing. Last night I spoke with a night-shift hotel maintenance worker. His name is Carmine. If he's not on your suspect list, add him."

"His name is Carmine Dumbrowski. He's on my list of people Charley targeted with an article."

Margaret slid from the booth and was gone in a matter of seconds. Fen turned to Lou. "I need you to pack and get to Fort Worth as soon as possible this morning. Go to the newspaper Charley worked at. Find out everything you can about him from the people he worked with. Get the personal stuff: habits, hobbies, relationships, what kind of car he drove, everything."

Lou tilted her head. "You want me to run from trouble? You know that's not how I'm wired."

"It's not running from trouble; it's running to information that can help us solve this case." He paused. "Excuse me. *These* cases. The more I think about it, the more I'm convinced they're linked. I'm also convinced we've worn out our welcome here. If it weren't for Hope being so busy with the Christmas parade, she'd spend more time making our lives miserable."

He didn't have time to expound on anything but a few parting comments. "Bailey and I will leave the hotel with you. You can drop us off at a car rental and I'll get something for us to get around in. That will keep my truck off the road and make Grimes's buddies think I'm holed up in my room."

Things were moving fast, which meant Lou had questions. Her training as a reporter made clarification a way of life for her. "Do you want me to sneak back here after I finish in Fort Worth?"

"Not back to the city. You may have to find a room in a neighboring county. We're less than twenty miles from the Oklahoma border. There are a couple of casinos with hotels not too far."

"Don't worry about me. I've dodged cops so many times I could teach a course on it."

"Me, too," said Bailey.

"Call Hap and see if Hope told the new sheriff to put a bounty on you, too. I hope we don't have to dodge cops outside the city limits, too."

"I'll call once I'm out of Wichita County." She took a last drink of coffee. "What are you going to do today?"

"I'm going to find out if Charley had life insurance, and if he did, who he named as the beneficiary."

"What about me?" asked Bailey.

"Sketches."

She looked into her coffee cup. "I got hung up on drawing an ear. Had to start over four or five times before I nailed it."

"That's your assignment for the day. Focus on Charley's eyes, nose, and mouth. I'm going to sketch Regina."

Lou scooted from the booth. "I'd prefer not to have a roadside talk with a cop this morning. My car will pull out of the parking lot in twenty minutes, with or without you."

"Come on, Bailey," said Fen. "We'll worry about breakfast later."

Fen had the sense they were getting close to a breakthrough. Lou and Bailey must have felt it, too. All three were walking to Lou's car with her luggage eighteen minutes after they left the restaurant. Bailey had even changed out of her fleece pajamas and put on jeans and a paint-stained, hooded sweatshirt.

A slight hiccup in Fen's plan occurred when he called car rental places and found they didn't open until 8:00 a.m. He and Bailey wished Lou a safe trip and went to Fen's truck. Once the diesel engine rattled to life, he looked at her. "We'll get a rental later today. It's more important that Lou get out of town as soon as possible."

Bailey looked at him. "Have you ever had to hide from the cops?"

"This is a first."

Bailey scanned the parking lot. "It's fun until they catch you."

"I'm not an expert at this kind of thing. How would you recommend we get from here to the university?"

"We're low priority. This is the time of day with the most traffic. The longer we stay on the main roads, the better the chance of them pulling us over."

"So we take the shortest route?"

"If they're really after us, they'll focus on the quickest route from the hotel to campus. We need to find the second or third fastest way." She paused. "I'll pull up a map program and give you directions." Bailey pointed. "Don't pull out on the main road in front of the hotel. Go to the back entrance. That's how Lou left."

She chuckled. "Once we get a rental car, we'll be fine. This truck sticks out like an elephant in a dog show."

Chapter Twenty-Two

The trip to campus went without a hitch, thanks to the route Bailey charted. They wove their way through neighborhoods, away from the primary arteries. It occurred to Fen how little attention the police paid to the side streets during periods of increased highway traffic. The lone exception was around neighborhood schools. Bailey avoided those, and they arrived safely on the MSU campus.

"Didn't I tell you?" said Bailey in a told-you-so voice.

"I say we were lucky. It's possible we wouldn't have passed a cop on any of the main roads, either. You never know when an accident or calls will keep the cops busy. Sometimes you'll see more than one on a brief trip. There's an old saying among police officers: 'You can definitely get away, but you can't get away indefinitely.'"

Bailey placed her scarred left hand on his arm. The wrinkled skin came from a burn she sustained shortly after they met. Her murdered uncle's body had washed up on Fen's property on the banks of the Brazos, which left her living alone in a dilapidated mobile home. An arsonist's fire almost took her life and led to a series of events that resulted in Fen solving the murder. In the end, he added a high school senior with exceptional talent to his unconventional family.

"Admit it," said Bailey. "It's a rush thinking the cops might come up behind you with red and blue lights flashing."

"I prefer to be the fox instead of the rabbit, but I have to admit, the trip to campus had my blood flowing."

The wind was picking up, as evidenced by leaves skip-dancing across the sidewalk. Fen took a firm grasp of the file folders he'd received from Margaret and Lou. He held them tight against his body as he and Bailey made their way from the faculty parking spaces and into the brick building. His commitment to proctor final exams for the Tuesday-Thursday classes would end today. Only one class tomorrow morning, and he'd be free to devote himself fully to the cases.

They stopped at the art professor's office and dropped off the files. He then led Bailey to the studio. She tilted her head as they walked down the empty hallway. "Why'd you bring files? I thought we were painting today."

"You're painting. I haven't had time to study all those documents. I'll be busy on that all day and into the night. Tomorrow, I'll sketch and paint."

Once in the studio, Bailey placed her sketch pad on a vacant easel and set her box of pencils on a table next to them. "Nice studio. Empty, but nice, and I'll be able to concentrate. Will any students be here with me?"

"It's possible. Some may come in and put final touches on Christmas presents they're making."

"I wonder how many parents have paintings their kids made for them, starting from the time they were big enough to hold a pencil or watercolor brush."

His thoughts went to his late wife and how they regretted their inability to have children of their own. The realization came to him that with Christmas right around the corner, he'd need to guard against the what-if's. They had a nasty habit of making special visits during holidays.

From their past conversations, he remembered Bailey had her own seasonal regrets, including a deceased father and an absentee mother. It was time to right his emotional ship.

"Let's go to the student union building and find something to eat. My first class isn't until nine-thirty."

They were rounding the corner of the building when Bailey pulled up short. He also stopped, and quizzed her with his stare. Following her gaze, they saw a city patrol car had pulled to a stop behind his truck.

Bailey stated the obvious. "That fox knows where the rabbit is hiding. All the foxes will know."

Fen's breath came out as a cloud as he huffed into the frosty morning air. "There's nothing he can do as long as the truck stays on university property and neither of us is driving."

"What about the university's police?"

"I'm sure Hope is a big donor, but I have a feeling she wants the city cops to nail us. I'm counting on her being too busy with the Christmas parade to not give us that much thought."

Bailey's phone rang. It took her a little longer than usual to retrieve it. She carried it in the back pocket of her jeans, covered by her sweatshirt and her winter coat. Puffy gloves had to be pulled off. After that, she had to snatch her wool cap off one ear. She announced, "It's Thelma. She calls me every morning. I'll put it on speaker so you can experience a slice of my world."

"What took you so long to answer?"

Bailey rolled her eyes. "I'm walking across campus with Fen. We're on our way to breakfast."

"Didn't that woman's cook fix you anything before sending you off into the snow?"

"There's no snow, only a stiff wind. That's what took me so long to answer. I'm bundled up like I'm running a pack of sled dogs."

"How are you feeling?"

"All well, and looking for a new boyfriend."

Fen covered a chuckle. Bailey was spoon-feeding news that would please Thelma.

"Good! I never trusted that shifty-eyed, skinny thing. You can do much better than him. How's Mr. Fen?"

"Oh, you know, he's all wrapped up in the case. He said we should finish in the next couple of weeks."

It was Bailey's turn to cover a laugh, which wasn't needed because Thelma's words exploded from the phone's speaker. "You tell that man he's to have you home no later than Sunday, or I'm coming back to that God-forsaken prairie and get you myself. Christmas ain't no time to be away from home."

Thelma took a breath and continued, "That police department has their own folks who are getting paid good money to solve crimes. They need to earn their keep without Mr. Fen having to carry their water for 'em."

Bailey must have known she'd breached a dam of pent-up emotions. She stemmed the flow of words by asking, "What's the latest in Newman County?"

Thelma knew everything private and public happening back home. Her voice filled with lament. "Nothing juicy. The biggest excitement we had was yesterday. Harley Cleaver forgot to put enough fuel in his airplane before taking off for his weekly breakfast in Fredericksburg. You know they got that parking lot for airplanes in front of an old-fashioned diner right off the runway. They tell me people fly in from all over. I guess that's what folks do when they have too much money.

They could eat a better omelet at home and save time and money."

Bailey interrupted. "What about not having enough gas? Was he killed? Anyone else hurt?"

"Don't get your knickers in a wad. I'm getting to that." She paused long enough to gather her thoughts. "Old Harley's been getting more and more forgetful with every year. It's a wonder he hasn't killed himself and taken half the county with him. Anyway, his plane ran out of fuel on the return trip and went straight into the roof of that new apartment complex they're building by the airport."

Thelma changed the tone of her voice and chased another proverbial rabbit. "Don't know why the county commissioners allowed them to build on the flight path to the airport. I knew it was only a matter of time before something like this would happen. If you ask me, those politicians need to spend less time in the coffee shop and more time—"

Bailey broke in again. "Was anyone killed?"

"Huh? No. Of course not. Harley flew that old plane into the roof and walked away without a scratch. They'd finished construction except for the carpet, so no one was living there. They had to get a crane to get the plane out of the attic."

"I bet that made front page news."

"Sure did. That reminds me. How's Lou?"

"On her way to Fort Worth to do more research on the case."

"Lord, have mercy. I won't sleep worth a plugged nickel until you all get home where you belong."

Bailey moved on, "How's Sam?"

"Giving me the silent treatment. He accused me of getting tipsy when I was taking care of you. I told him it was the cough medicine that made me a little wobbly. I was fine until I took the store-bought stuff."

Bailey winked and spoke in a sympathetic tone. "Some people jump to conclusions. I remember you telling me it's our duty to forgive them. Tell Sam I miss him and that I want to go hunting when I get home."

"That will thrill him so much he might even smile." She hesitated, but not for long. "You're right about forgiving people. Hope Ellison is at the top of my list. That woman has a short fuse and jumps to conclusions. I was glad to put her place in my rearview mirror."

"I think Fen and I have had our fill, too. I'm looking forward to getting home."

"Remember what I said about you being here by Sunday. I mean it."

"I'll tell Fen that lumps of coal will be the only thing in his stocking if we're not on the road by noon on Sunday."

The call ended, and Fen crammed his hands deeper into the pockets of his coat. "There are very few people who can handle Thelma the way you do. You gave her just enough information to satisfy her, cut her off when she rambled, and even found out the big news back home."

She tugged the wool cap back down over her ears. "I'm turning into a block of ice. Let's step it up and find some hot chocolate."

It was Fen's turn to receive a call. The screen on his phone read Chuck Forsythe, his attorney.

"Bad news travels on wings," mumbled Fen.

Bailey shivered. "Huh?"

"Nothing. Get inside and put something hot in your belly."

He didn't need to tell her twice. Bailey was pulling the door open by the time he answered his phone. He took in a deep breath and activated the device. "Good morning, Chuck."

"What have you done?"

Chapter Twenty-Three

Chuck Forsythe and Fen went back a long way. The attorney was one of the most unflappable men he'd ever met. Today, however, he was flapping.

"What in the world did you do to Hope? Of all the people in Wichita County, why did you pick her as an enemy?"

"It was a series of unfortunate circumstances."

"That's an understatement. How are you planning on solving the case when you're in a jail cell?"

"It's not that bad." A doubt passed through his mind. "At least I don't think it's that bad. It was Lou's stories in the Dallas and Fort Worth newspapers that pushed Hope over the edge."

Chuck shot back, "Newspapers? She fed the story to television stations! That woman is amazing, and not in a good way."

Fen caught himself nodding as he spoke. "Yeah, but you have to understand how Hope and Lou see themselves. Lou believes in total transparency and let the chips fall where they may."

He took a quick breath. "On the other hand, Hope believes

she's the guardian angel over the county and is super-sensitive about the press carrying anything but positive news."

"She probably has enough pull to buy an angel or two. I still haven't heard a good reason to explain why you crossed swords with her."

Fen had heard enough. "Look, Chuck. I'm close to solving both cases. I can feel it. Lou's on her way to Fort Worth to interview people who knew the murder victim. I told her to stay clear of Wichita County."

"Murder? Your job is to find Regina and try to get back a pile of money. Let the locals solve the murder."

"I'm convinced the two cases are glued so tightly together we can't pull them apart. Detective Margaret Sibley and her father, the former sheriff, are still helping me."

"How? From what I hear, the chief of police told everyone in his department that they're to treat you like you have leprosy."

"Good. That means they'll leave me alone."

Candy's voice came next. "Fen. You need to excuse Chuck. He's the only person in the world that loves Christmas fruit cake. It's been soaking in brandy for three weeks. Last night he ate a third of it and his tummy is giving him fits this morning."

"There's nothing wrong with my bowels," shouted Chuck.

Fen couldn't help but laugh.

Candy ignored both the laugh and her husband. "Give us an update. Are things as hopeless as Chuck thinks?"

It was good to hear Candy's calm voice. Fen took in a full breath and launched into what he hoped would sound like an optimistic conclusion to the cases. "Like I said, Lou's out of harm's way. Hope is running herself ragged keeping the Christmas parade on track. Bailey is with me, all healed and whole."

"Is she helping with the investigation?" asked Chuck.

"She is, but I'm keeping her out of any sort of compromising position. She'll complete sketches this morning of Charley Cleg's facial features. If you don't remember, he's the murder victim."

"I remember. How will that help you find Regina?"

"It probably won't, but she was feeling better and I needed to keep her busy. I'm teaching Bailey how to lose herself in thought as she draws and paints."

"That sounds like new-age nonsense," said Chuck with a low grumble in his voice.

Candy spoke over her husband, "Keep going, Fen."

"I have three files. They contain all the information collected by the former sheriff, his daughter Margaret, and Lou's research. Today and tonight, I'll review every scrap of information collected on Regina, Charley, and every victim of Regina's scam."

"And then?" asked Chuck.

"Lou will add to the pile with what she finds out in Fort Worth today. Tomorrow, I'll sketch and think. It's when I'm lost in art that answers come to me. When that happens, we find Regina, get the money back, and solve a murder."

"What happens if the answers don't come?" asked Chuck.

"Then we all come home on Saturday, and give the job of finding both Regina and the person who murdered Charley back to the police."

"I don't like the second choice. Work on the first and throw in repairing our relationship with Hope as a bonus."

Candy spoke with confidence. "I believe in you, Fen. If anyone can put the pieces together, it's you."

"A couple more things," said Fen. "Bailey and I are leaving my truck here on campus and getting a rental car to get around. Margaret is updating financial statements on the primary suspects. She's also tracking down life insurance policies on

Charley. It will be interesting to see who he named as his bene-ficiary."

"Do me a favor," said Chuck. "Stay out of jail."

"That's what I have Bailey for. Her experience of outsmarting the Houston cops brings a different perspective to investigations."

Chuck groaned. "Wichita Falls isn't as big as Houston. Fewer places to hide."

The call cut off.

Once inside the student union building, Fen looked for Bailey. She came to him holding two paper cups. "I got you coffee and hot chocolate for me."

"Perfect. Let's find something to eat."

Before they could take a step, Fen's phone rang again. Lou's name appeared. A sinking feeling hit him. "Please tell me you're not in jail."

"Sorry to disappoint you, but I made it out of Wichita County with no trouble other than having to take back roads. I'm coming up on Decatur, where I'll stop for breakfast."

"That's what Bailey and I are about to do. We made it to campus without getting busted. A city cop spotted my truck, so we're stuck here. I'll call and see if I can get a rental car deliv-ered to the university. It shouldn't be a problem."

"Good thinking."

"It was Bailey's idea. She has a full bag of tricks to get past the police. I'm the student, and she's the teacher today."

"We all have our talents, and speaking of, I made an appointment with the editor of the Fort Worth newspaper Charley worked for. He said he'll introduce me to the people who worked with him."

"What did that cost you?"

"A full recounting of the story after you solve it."

"Nothing like a little pressure. Have you decided where you'll spend the night?"

"Hold on! I almost missed my exit."

Tires squealed, and a horn honked.

"That was close. What did you ask?"

"Where are you staying tonight?"

"After I'm finished at the newspaper, I'm heading back to Wichita County." She moved on before he could interrupt. "Before you tell me I can't, it's all arranged. I'll bypass the four-lane and go on backroads to Hap's. He gave me a route that's rarely patrolled. I'll park in his barn and stay in the guest bedroom. If I need to come to town, I'll ride with him."

Fen looked for flaws in the plan and found the risk acceptable. "I guess that leaves you free to ride horses again."

"Not unless it warms up."

He couldn't help but notice the lift in Lou's voice. Chasing down stories was her vocation and passion. He wasn't sure how chasing a former sheriff compared, but he was sure it gave a boost to her Christmas. "Call me with a report as soon as you're finished at the newspaper."

"Will do. Listen to Bailey when you leave campus today. She has tricks up her sleeves that will surprise you."

Following a quick breakfast, Fen and Bailey braved the elements and returned to the world of art. They'd used up their words over breakfast and walked in silence.

They arrived, and Fen went back to the office. Before reviewing files, his thoughts went back to Bailey. In some ways, they mirrored each other in personality. Long hours alone didn't bother them a bit, but they could come out of their shells to interact at a moment's notice. She'd proven herself to be a valuable assistant on previous cases.

He dismissed the thoughts and opened the thickest of the

three files. Well-rested and full of caffeine, he focused on well-thumbed pages. What had Hap and Margaret missed?

Bailey appeared in the doorway of his borrowed office at 12:05 p.m. "I'm going to get a chicken sandwich. Do you want anything?"

Fen kept his head down. "Spicy chicken sandwich with waffle fries and a diet Coke." He reached for his wallet and extracted a credit card. "Be sure to get a receipt."

"How many times have you reminded me to get receipts?"

"Business expenses."

"I know. I have to file taxes, too. Keep your credit card. I need the tax write-off."

He grunted and went back to reading.

She returned from lunch with plenty of time for him to eat before his afternoon class. The files went to one side of the desk and made room for his meal. The trip across campus lowered the temperature of the meal to tepid. They ate without talking until all that remained were a few cool waffle fries.

"How are the sketches coming?"

"I'm finished with the individual facial features. I guess I'll start on the portrait."

He leaned back in his chair. "That may not be necessary. I have something else for you to work on."

"What's that?"

"Let me look at the sketches before I tell you."

Bailey spoke with confidence. "They're good. I used photos that Lou got from the newspaper. I even got the ears right."

Fen stood. "Let's look."

The clip-clop of his boots echoed in the hall on the way to the studio. A pair of students stood in front of easels with the corners of their mouths dipped in a frown.

"What's wrong?" asked Fen.

"My mom's mouth looks like a worm."

The second student said, "The angle of my dad's eyebrows makes him look like a mad scientist."

Fen turned to Bailey. "You work on the mouth. I'll help with the eyebrows."

Bailey grabbed her sketch pad while Fen asked his student to flip his pad to a clean sheet. He listened as Bailey made the first strokes of showing her student how to draw a mouth. "The key is to think in three dimensions. Watch as I make an outline of the mouth. Notice that I'm only putting what's the most distant. Think of your strokes as building a sculpture of clay. Focus on the photo until you see the layers."

"What do you mean, layers?"

"Distance. What's closest to you and what's farthest?"

Fen looked at his student. "Are you listening to her?"

"Yeah. I'm listening and watching. She's good. Real good."

"You can be, too, if you think in layers. I'll show you."

It wasn't a race, so both allowed their student to progress at their own pace. Drawing layer upon layer, they soon had acceptable representations of the lips and eyebrows of the people in their photos.

"Very good," said Fen. "Use that same method on your portrait in paint, and your parents will think you're a genius."

"Mine knows better," said the student, who frowned at the eyebrows.

"Another trick," said Fen. "Draw them the way they think they look, which is usually better than they do. Faces are imperfect, but that isn't the way people want theirs to look. It doesn't hurt to fudge on the side of flattery, especially with parents. That's why photographers airbrush to soften photos."

The second student laughed. "Never trust a photo on a dating site."

Bailey gave her head a firm nod. "I learned that lesson the hard way."

It was news to Fen, but he didn't have time to dwell on it. "You two keep working on your portraits. Bailey needs to show me what she's been working on."

"Can we look?"

"Sure," said Bailey. She put her sketches on the easel. "These are individual facial features."

"They look real," said the first student.

Fen rubbed his chin. "They're supposed to. Unlike your portraits, these portray stark realism."

Bailey took over while he tuned out the voices, focused on the photos, and compared them to her sketches. Something important was trying to rise to the surface, but he couldn't grasp it. There was something very familiar about the individual facial features. The student's voices broke the spell. All that remained was the feeling he'd swung and missed a fat pitch right down the middle of the plate.

He pulled Bailey over to another easel and uncovered his partially completed canvas. "I have a lot to do and our days are running out. I'd like for you to start on Regina's portrait today."

Bailey looked at him in surprise. "Okay, but I won't have time to get very far today."

Perhaps tomorrow, when he could dedicate himself to his partially completed work, he'd get another chance to hit a home run.

Chapter Twenty-Four

F en huffed his way back to the office, hoping the near miss on the revelation that would solve the cases would make a repeat appearance.

Bailey stayed in the studio, adding Regina's face to the two images of the waterfall and the tiny skyscraper. It was supposed to be his painting, but he needed to focus first on the information contained in the thick files.

While rubbing his eyes, his phone signaled an incoming call. He glanced down as it vibrated on the desk and saw Margaret's name. He hoped she'd been productive in chasing down the financial status of a handful of people. His hopes soon lay in shattered pieces.

"Listen close," said Margaret. "Jay is coordinating a plan to arrest Bailey tonight."

The words caused Fen to take all the slack out of his spine. "I thought the chief suspended him."

"He did, but with pay. The plan is for Larry Fry and some good old boys to come to her room. He'll say he has some follow-up questions for her."

Fen could see what would unfold. "Then they'll say she became belligerent. She'll go in cuffs with an assault on a peace officer charge. It will be the words of three cops against a cocky young woman who's already shown aggression."

Margaret didn't contradict him, so Fen took a few seconds to think. "Grimes is after you, not Bailey. If you get involved, you'll play into his plan of getting you fired or demoted. Stay clear of this. I'll think of something."

"You'd better think fast. They're keeping a sharp eye on your truck. They want to wait until the top brass go home for the day before they come to your hotel."

"Thanks for the warning. Did you work on the financial reports and insurance beneficiary?"

"I got started, but still have a long way to go."

"Keep at it. I'll be at the university again tomorrow unless they arrest me."

"The word is you're off limits until Sunday at noon. I think Jay's plan is to keep Bailey in jail long enough that you'll stick around past the weekend. Then his minions will come after you."

He was going to say something pithy, but nothing came to mind. Margaret ended the call with a quick, "Got to go. Be careful."

Fen shoved his phone into the pocket of his vest and hustled to the studio. Bailey stood in front of an easel, so focused on her work that she didn't acknowledge his presence. He stood in front of her and cleared his throat. "Earth to Bailey."

She shook her head. "Sorry. I was practicing what you told me about getting lost in thought while I work."

"That's good, but we have a problem. The police are planning to arrest you tonight."

"Wow! That's amazing. This thinking and painting thing

really works." A broad smile pulled her lips apart. "Don't worry, I'll be fine."

Fen shook his head. "I don't think you understand. They're going to come under the pretext of asking questions and provoke you into saying or doing something."

"Yeah, I know. But I won't be around to arrest."

Fen looked at her with brows raised. "How do you know, and where will you be?"

"Sorry. I can't tell you. It's time for you to trust me."

Fen tried to think of ways she could hide. Nothing foolproof came to mind. "They're monitoring my truck, so you trying to leave the county isn't an option. You're not allowed to drive the rental car, so that's out. They'll find you if you stay in another hotel, and getting a flight or a bus out of town is too dicey."

She waved away his words. "Don't worry. I have everything set up."

Fen couldn't believe her calm demeanor. "What's your plan?"

"Can't tell you. If I do, you'd have to lie to the police."

Frustration enveloped him like a blanket. His voice raised in pitch. "If this plan of yours involves Lou, you can forget it. They're looking for her, too."

"It doesn't involve Lou, but I'll call her when I get to where I'm going tonight. Don't call or text. All you need to do is trust me."

Fen didn't like the way she'd painted him into a corner by playing the trust card. He filled his lungs. "Can you at least give me the first part of your plan?"

Her hair bounced as she nodded. "I'll go to the student union building as soon as it's dark, walk straight through, and go out another door. I'll make sure nobody follows me and disappear into the night. Shaking a tail isn't that hard."

She grinned. "There can't be more than two of Grimes's buddies watching us, and they're expecting us to stay together and take your truck back to the hotel or to supper. You had the rental delivered to a different parking lot. By the time they figure out you have a rental and I'm not in my room, I'll be long gone."

It was obvious she'd put a lot more thought into them avoiding the cops than he had. She was on a roll, so he let her talk.

"Leave your cowboy hat here and put my sock cap on when you leave. If you can stand to be cold, leave your coat in the office, too. Go out through a different door and slouch when you walk. Hop in the rental and go straight to the hotel."

Fen looked for flaws in her plan. The only one he saw was that he didn't know where she planned to go and how she would get there. He opened his mouth to speak, but she cut him off.

"Don't worry about me. I'll be safer than you."

He sighed in resignation. "All right. You've been playing the role of a rabbit longer than me."

She motioned for him to come to her side of the easel. He took the steps and stared at the drawing. It was an excellent start, but needed work.

"I'll continue to work on Regina's facial features, but won't have time to draw her chin, hair or throat. I hope it will be enough. My sketch pad is staying here. If someone's watching, I want them to think I'm going for something to eat and coming back."

He moved back to get a different perspective. "This is excellent work."

"Thanks. Go back to the office and don't worry about me. It's best you don't know when I leave."

He knew he'd worry but mouthed words of assurance

anyway. Back in the office, he resumed studying the contents of the files. It was at least forty minutes after dark when he checked the art studio. Bailey's sketch pad and pencils were the only sign she'd ever been there.

The wool cap warmed his ears on the way to the rental. The temperature was falling fast, and his nose dripped by the time he clicked the key fob and entered the sub-compact. Thrift had won out over comfort. Besides, who would expect to see him in such a tiny gas-sipper?

After an uneventful drive, the rental slid between white lines at the side of the hotel. His key card allowed him to enter through a side door, avoiding the front desk. He took the stairs to his floor and was in his room after passing no one. So far, so good.

His thoughts fixed on Bailey. Where was she? Who was she with? He kicked off his boots and placed the three files on the bed. He'd finish reading and making notes on Hap's massive accumulation of information after supper.

Going to the dining room alone didn't appeal to him, so he turned on the television, muted the sound, and found the room service menu. A quick phone call later and he was told to expect delivery of a sandwich in about twenty-five minutes.

Pounding on the door came soon after he ordered. He had a feeling it wasn't room service. The view from the peep hole revealed two cops in uniform and Larry Fry looking ridiculous in a Dick Tracy trench coat over what looked like a cheap suit.

The frame of the door had a metal security device that, when engaged, allowed only a three-inch gap. It was much stronger than the chains some hotels used. Fen waited until Fry banged on the door again before moving the slab of metal to the secure position.

Fen spoke in a normal voice. "Who is it?"

"Police. Open up, Maguire."

Fen did as instructed, but not as expected. The door came to a sudden stop.

"I said open up."

"What do you want?"

His question must have taken the trio by surprise. Fen watched through the opening as they held a brief meeting and discussed what to do.

Fry returned. "Where's the girl?"

"What girl?"

"That Madison Bailey girl."

"Her first name is Bailey, and the last name is Madison."

"Whatever. Where is she?"

"Have you checked her room?"

"Yeah. She ain't there. That means she's with you."

Fen was enjoying this. "She's nineteen. I don't keep track of her every move. Did you check the dining room?"

"Yeah. And the pool, and the business office, and the..."

Fry shouted, "Never mind where we looked. She's in there with you."

"I already told you she isn't here."

"We don't believe you."

"Have you ever known me to lie?"

"I'm through playing games with you. Let us in or go to jail."

Fen didn't want to press his luck too far but didn't mind making them wait. "All right, keep your shirt on. I have nothing to hide. Give me a minute." He shut the door but left the security device engaged.

The three file folders went into a pillowcase, leaving no room for the pillow. He laid the pillow on a shelf in the top of the clothes closet. After examining the room, he nodded with satisfaction and moved to the door.

He disengaged the security latch and opened the door. "Come in, gentleman."

All three breezed past him. One peeled off and went into the bathroom. The sound of the shower curtain being jerked back flowed into the bedroom area. An announcement followed, "She's not in here."

Fen passed Larry Fry, went to the bed, and lay with his back against two pillows. The first was down-filled, while the one containing the files leaned between the backboard and the pillow. "I told you she wasn't here."

"There's nothing wrong with our eyes. We can see she ain't here. But we all have ears, and you're going to tell us where she is."

"I can't tell what I don't know."

"All right. Where do you think she might be?" He paused. "Or don't you want to help the police with a murder investigation?"

"You have no idea how much I want to help. In fact, I'll start right now. Did you know Bailey and J.W. Ellison have a romantic thing going on?"

Officer Fry's head wagged like the tail of a dog. "You're behind the times. Mrs. Ellison put a stop to that when she kicked you out of her home."

Fen shrugged. "You're probably right. Bailey worked all day in the art studio at MSU. Have you checked there?"

Muscles in Fry's cheeks flexed as he ground his molars and refused to answer.

At least twenty seconds of silence followed before one of the other officers said, "It's possible he's telling the truth. I think we should look for J.W.'s truck. I never did what my mom told me to do when I was chasing girls."

A knock on the door sounded. Two of the three placed

their hands on the grip of their pistols. The words "Room service" came from the hallway.

"That's my supper," said Fen. "If you want to stick around, I'll see if they'll bring a pot of coffee up."

The three traded glances, and Fry snapped his head toward the door. They filed past the server, who watched the parade with wide eyes.

Fen was halfway through his sandwich when it occurred to him that he may have told the police how to find Bailey. She may have recruited J.W. to pick her up at MSU. He considered calling her, but that would telegraph mistrust. Besides, he doubted Larry Fry and his two buddies had the cunning to outfox her. Suspended detective Jay Grimes was a different story, but his money was still on Bailey to elude the foxes.

Chapter Twenty-Five

F en had always been an early riser, even as a child. His twenty years in law enforcement had trained him to get by on little sleep, which was a good thing on this winter's morning. Reading, taking notes, and putting together clues from the mounds of information had lasted until 1:30 a.m. His internal alarm clock went off at 5:00 a.m., the same time as usual.

The hotel room's two-cup coffee maker spit and sputtered out black stimulant. As was his custom, he put his phone on silent, retrieved Sally's five-by-seven framed photo, and gave her a report of yesterday's activities. He followed this with a monologue of what he hoped to accomplish today. Her presence was with him every morning. Sometimes he could swear she spoke to him, but not today.

The talk lasted longer than normal as reports meshed together and patterns developed. Still, a sizeable gap remained unfilled. He hoped yesterday's efforts from Lou and Margaret would reap rewards.

"It's time for me to get ready for the day, sweetheart. Love you and miss you so much."

It was a standard salutation, but no matter how many times he recited it, the words stuck in his throat.

A glance at his phone showed nothing yet from Lou or Margaret, but Hope had left three messages. "Might as well get this over with."

The phone was completing its first ring when Hope demanded, "Where's my son and that tramp?"

Fen pushed the red icon, cutting off the call. He then muted the phone and padded to the bathroom to shower and shave. A grin remained as he smeared shaving gel across his whisker-stubbled face. He was right. Bailey had called J.W. So far, they'd eluded Hope and the police. It didn't answer where they'd escaped to, but it led him to believe J.W. had more backbone than he thought.

After dressing, Fen placed a call to Hope. Like before, she answered on the first ring. "Don't you ever hang up on me aga—"

He did and waited for her to call him back. When she did, he spoke before she had a chance to. "I haven't seen Bailey since yesterday afternoon. I don't have any idea where she went or who she's with. Act like a mature adult, or don't call me again."

Ice was in her voice. "I don't believe you."

He'd determined when he was showering not to fall into the trap of arguing with her, so he said nothing.

"I know they're together."

Silence.

She sprayed the next words as if they came from a water gun. "I care deeply for my son. If you had a child, you'd understand. That little witch has cast some sort of spell on him."

No response.

"Say something!"

"I already have. I don't know where they are or if they're together."

"That's not good enough."

"Then call the police and report J.W. missing."

"I already have. They're worthless."

The beeps in his ear notified him of an incoming call. "Hold on, Bailey's calling me now." He put Hope on hold.

Bailey sounded chipper. "Good morning. I'm not interrupting your time with Sally, am I?"

"Not at all. I have Hope on hold. She's ready to call out the National Guard to find you two."

"She's wasting her time. I wanted to let you know we're safe and sound. I knew she'd call the cops."

"Is J.W. with you now?"

"He's in his room. I haven't spoken to him this morning."

"Have him call his mom this morning, preferably as soon as possible."

"Will do. Lou found some interesting things about Charley. I spoke with her last night and I'll call Thelma in a few minutes." She paused. "Are we still leaving town tomorrow?"

He poured another cup of coffee as he answered. "Either tomorrow afternoon or Sunday morning. It all depends if I can make sense of these goofy cases."

"Either you or Lou may have to come get me. I'm not sure if J.W. can stand up to his mother much longer."

"I'd better go. Hope may strip a gear if I leave her on hold much longer."

Bailey's giggle assured him he'd been right to trust her.

The call switched back to Hope. He spoke in quick, short bursts. "J.W. is safe. Bailey didn't tell me where they were. It's a place where they stayed in separate rooms."

"Didn't you ask where?"

"No."

"Why not?"

"I trust her."

"Bull. What else did she say?"

"We talked briefly about the cases we're working on. I told her to tell J.W. to call you as soon as she talked to him."

"Is that all?"

"She wanted to know when we were leaving town."

"Not soon enough."

Silence.

Frustration colored her words. "Of all times for J.W. to pull a stunt like this. The stupid parade is falling apart, and he's acting like he has no responsibility to the community. He's just like his father... and you."

The call cut off. Fen looked at it and said, "That explains a lot." His stomach interrupted his thoughts with a gurgle. Time for breakfast; a busy day awaited him.

He pulled on his boots and gathered everything needed for the day, including the three files and his notes. Unlike last night, he used the elevator and headed for the dining room. After considering the selections, he chose the three-egg western omelet and biscuits. That would hold him all day then he'd be able to lose himself in completing the portrait of Regina.

He polished off the last bite of gravy-covered biscuit when Lou called. Fen looked at the time on his phone. It was earlier than normal for Lou.

"Good morning." Like Bailey, Lou's voice had a cheerful tone to it. He hoped that meant she'd had a productive day in Fort Worth.

"I guess there's no sleeping late on a ranch." He pushed the almost empty plate to the opposite side of the table. "Bailey called a while ago. She said you scored some good information in Fort Worth."

"Uh-huh. It seems Charley was a one-hit-wonder."

"What does that mean?"

Instead of Lou answering, Hap's voice came over the phone from what sounded like the other side of a room. "Good morning, Fen. Did you get anything of value from my file?"

"The pieces are coming together. I'm hoping what you tell me will bring everything into focus. Is Margaret listening, too?"

"She's up, dressed, and gone. Said she'd call you today and give a full report on the suspect's finances."

"Good. Lou, what did you find out about Charley?"

"I spoke to the editor. He passed me off to a couple of reporters who worked with Charley. It seems he was a disappointment. His stories were nothing like those he wrote in Wichita Falls. Most of his research came from computer searches. No depth and poor follow-up with sources. He produced nothing that an intern couldn't do. They described him as lazy."

"Were his stories as caustic as the ones he wrote about the people here?"

"Both reporters I talked to described them as stories without teeth. I read several, and they're right. He had good leads on a couple of scandals and didn't even ask the main characters for comments. Hope would have loved the way he wrote them."

"I don't get it. He was vicious with the people here. Did he lose his nerve?"

Hap's words interrupted them. "Can I give you a warm-up on that coffee?"

"Please," said Lou in a coy voice.

Any thoughts of Lou not enjoying her time with Hap melted away like morning frost in warm sunshine.

"Where was I?"

Fen couldn't help but smile. "You were telling me how Charley's personality changed."

"Yeah, yeah. It was like he turned into a different man. No killer instinct."

Fen was processing the drastic change in the reporter when Lou continued, "I asked the reporters if Charley was free with his money. That got a reaction from both of them, but not like I thought. They said he was a tightwad, even though it was an open secret that he'd landed a hefty salary. He drove a ratty old Honda Civic that sounded like it suffered from emphysema." She paused. "Their words, not mine."

"I would have thought he'd have new wheels and lived in a swinging bachelor pad."

"That made me curious, so I found out where he lived. The police had sealed the one-bedroom apartment and were taking down the crime scene tape when I arrived. The forensic team didn't rush to process his place because the murder took place in Wichita Falls." She paused. "I might have given them the impression that I was the property manager."

Fen raised his voice. "Watch her close, Hap. She's sneaky."

"I've got both eyes on her."

He knew what Hap meant, and it didn't pertain to the case. "What was his apartment like?"

"Boring. It was furnished in early-marriage, except for a gigantic television. I found enough make-up to convince me he had an infrequent lady visitor. It was a cheap brand, so I doubt it belongs to his ex-wife. You described her as somewhat narcissistic."

"I'm no expert, but she doesn't skimp on looking her best. Did the reporters you spoke with mention anything about his love life?"

"Not a word, and I asked. He guarded his personal life like

it was a state secret. That's hard to do when you work with nosy reporters."

Fen took in the information. It was like the separate pieces of Bailey's sketches of Charley's face. How did they fit together?

"Did you find anything that surprised you?"

"Golf clubs. Not just any clubs, but the most expensive you can buy. I took a photo of them and stopped at a specialty golf shop. It's amazing how much you can spend hitting a little white ball."

Fen leaned back in the booth. "Golf clubs? I don't associate investigative reporters with golf clubs."

"Me either, but there they were in the hall closet. So were golf shoes and a collection of hats from courses all over, even a few from fancy destinations out of state."

"That would explain some of what he spent his money on."

"One more thing," said Lou. "The editor told me he was planning on giving Charley his pink slip after the new year."

"Another surprise." Fen slid out of the booth. "You've given me plenty to think about. I spoke with Bailey this morning. Don't worry, I won't ask you where she is."

"She's having a great time." Lou waited a tick of the clock before asking, "Have you heard from Hope?"

"Oh, yeah. She's learning to let go of J.W. the hard way."

He could see in his mind's eye Lou holding up her hand. "That's all I need to know. In fact, that's more than I want to know about that woman."

"I'll be at the university if you need me. One more final exam and the rest of the day I'll be working on a portrait of Regina."

"I thought you'd already done that."

"I've been busy trying to keep people out of jail. So busy, in fact, that I had Bailey start on the portrait."

Hap's voice came over the phone. "I sure appreciate every-thing you're doing."

The call came to a close, and his thoughts shifted to Hap's daughter, Margaret. What would she add to the piles of information?

Chapter Twenty-Six

The art studio seemed colder than usual when Fen arrived. He blamed it on having only his vest to wear over a shirt as he trekked from a distant parking lot. At least his hands had remained warm in the pockets of his vest. He went to the office and retrieved his coat.

The wool cap and coat came off after fifteen minutes, leaving him with static-laden hat hair. Oh well, at least he could finally work on Regina's likeness. Before starting on the third image, he inspected what he and Bailey had completed so far. The waterfall and tiny skyscraper looked amateurish, but they sufficed for his purpose. No way he'd sign this slapped-together work.

He pulled photos of Regina from the inside pocket of his coat. Lou obtained them from the local newspaper, and he'd forgotten to ask if they wanted them back. He'd mail them after he completed the portrait.

It was a relief to concentrate on the sketch. One thing after another had kept him from drawing Regina. Light strokes from a pencil left faint marks on the page as he picked up where

Bailey left off. He hoped he had enough time to give a decent effort in capturing the woman who'd caused so much grief.

It was almost ten before he realized what time it was; he needed to pass out the last final exam. The pencils went back into their box and he hurried to the office, then to the class-room. Only a handful of students were there to take the test, as most of the class had done well enough to be exempt from the final. The brevity of the test allowed him to get back to his drawing.

He could now devote himself fully to Regina's portrait and get into an uninterrupted time alone. He stood before the easel, said a brief prayer, and tried to clear his mind. It took two hours of drawing before his brain disconnected from a series of rambling thoughts. The scratching on the page melted away until he couldn't hear it. This was the prelude to flow.

The door to the art studio flung open and banged against the wall with a resounding crack. Flow-state took wings. He ground his teeth in anger as he looked up to find the offender, then ground them more when he saw who it was.

"There you are," declared Jay Grimes. "You thought you could hide from me by getting a rental car."

"Yeah," said Larry Fry as he followed Grimes like a tag-along, obnoxious little brother.

Fen turned away from the pair, put his phone on the easel, and started recording. More than anything, he collected his thoughts and waited for the pair to make fools of themselves. It didn't take long.

"Turn around when I'm talking to you, Maguire," said Grimes.

Fen stood to the side so his camera could get a clear shot. He took his time in facing them and said, "Does the chief know you're here?"

"What he don't know won't hurt him. Besides, you know he don't run nothin'."

"If you say so. What do you want?"

"Where's J.W. and that smart-mouthed girl?"

"Lou Cooper?"

"No, wise guy. Not the reporter. The young one that should be in jail."

"I know nothing about a young girl that should be in jail. Who are you talking about?"

"That Madison Bailey girl," said Fry with thumbs hooked on his belt.

Fen feigned surprise. "Oh! You mean Bailey Madison. You still have her first and last name mixed up. It's easy to do."

"I thought it was the other way."

"Shut up, Larry. I'll handle this." Grimes fixed his gaze on Fen. "Where are they?"

"I haven't seen her since yesterday afternoon. Did you check her room again this morning?"

"You're testing my patience, which isn't a smart thing to do. She went into the student union building yesterday and didn't come out."

"Did she?"

"You know she did. If you want to pretend you don't know where she is, we can play the same game with you."

"No, thanks. I'm not much on playing games."

"You'd better do as Detective Grimes says," said Fry. "We don't want you to wind up with a broken nose like Mason Cleg. You're lying, and we know it."

"That's quite an accusation. Can you prove it?"

Grimes shouted, "I'm the one asking questions!"

"I only cooperate with police officers in good standing. You're suspended." He then smiled at Larry. "Why don't you do the asking, Officer Fry?"

"Mrs. Ellison is on us like stink on a skunk. She told the chief—"

"Shut up, Larry." Crimson crept up Grimes's face.

Fen's phone rang.

"Don't answer it," commanded Grimes.

Fen already had the phone to his ear. "Hello, Margaret. I'm glad you called. Jay and Larry are here. They're asking me where J.W. Ellison and Bailey are."

"What! Put the phone on speaker."

Fen pushed the icon. "Your senior partner wants to talk to you, Larry."

The tone of Margaret's words brooked no dispute. "Larry, you called in sick today. You've sure had a miraculous recovery. If you're not in my office in five minutes, you'll be riding a stick horse checking parking meters downtown."

Fen spoke in a loud voice, "Don't tell her you came to my hotel room last night with two other officers."

He could only imagine what Margaret's face looked like as her next words seethed out. "Larry, you now have four minutes to be in my office."

His Adam's apple bobbed up and back down. "Yes, ma'am. I'm on my way."

"You're not going anywhere," said Grimes.

Larry Fry turned and made tracks to the door while speaking over his shoulder. "Forget it, Jay. I have a wife and kids to think about. From now on, you're on your own."

"Fen," said Margaret. "Should I contact the chief or bypass him and go straight to the Texas Rangers?"

"It's your call."

A few seconds of silence passed before she asked if he was recording the conversation.

"I certainly am."

"Are you armed?"

"Aren't all former sheriffs?"

"That sounds like a yes to me."

Fen thought he knew what Margaret wanted and said, "I'll stop the recording. You have plenty to nail Jay to the wall if you want to."

A few seconds of silence passed. He turned off the recording and went back to the call.

"I'm no longer recording."

"Jay, can you hear me?" asked Margaret.

"Yeah. You'll regret this."

A few more long seconds passed.

Margaret heaved a sigh. "Fen, don't kill him, but I don't care if you shoot him in the other arm or just break it."

"That's the best offer I've had since I arrived."

In a matter of seconds, Fen stood alone in the art studio. That was the good news. The bad was that he could forget about returning to flow-state anytime soon. He was so close to solving the cases he could almost taste it. There was only one thing left to do. Get back to drawing and hope for a miracle.

Chapter Twenty-Seven

Try as he might, Fen couldn't return to the groove he was in prior to Grimes's arrival in the studio. There remained a deep chasm between the answers to the cases and where he stood. He stared at his and Bailey's drawing with two parts completed and one unfinished. He then examined Bailey's renderings of Charley's facial features. Frustration bubbled up.

There was nothing he could do but follow the instruction he'd given Bailey. Perhaps if he just kept going on the sketch, something would come to him. He stared at a photograph of Regina. His focus fixed on the triangle of her eyebrows down to her bottom lip. "Focus on the details," said Fen to himself. "It may take me the rest of the day and all night, but I'm going to complete this."

The afternoon slipped into early evening. He'd worked his way from eyebrows to the top lip when his phone rang again. He'd wanted to put it on silent, but concern for Bailey and Margaret's promise to call him if she found anything else of interest changed his mind.

"Are you still at the art studio?" asked Margaret after they exchanged greetings.

"Still here. Please tell me you've come up with something useful."

"I wish I could. I've spent all day going over the bank records of all the prime suspects. Carmine Dumbrowski was the last. Nothing of significance. He's digging out from under a mountain of debt. His motive for killing Charley is strong, but forty or fifty other people share the same sentiment."

"Nothing else?"

"I thought I had something, but it turned out to be a dead end. There was a hundred grand in-and-out on Charley's bank statement. When he first moved to Fort Worth, he purchased a rental home north of the city."

"That sounds like a smart investment. I didn't have Charley pictured as a landlord. Anything else?"

"Hope's bank account fluctuates widely, but when you're dealing with that many millions of dollars, it's not unusual. Oil prices cause wild swings in revenue. The same with cattle. A three-hundred-thousand-dollar loss in real estate is like a pimple on an elephant."

Fen agreed in part, but he'd seen the controlling side of Hope on full display. She could and would have made life miserable for Charley if given the chance.

His next words were a question he'd been wrestling with for some time. "Something's been bothering me. Why did Charley return to Wichita Falls?"

"Didn't Lou tell you? Fellow reporters in Fort Worth said he was writing a tell-all book about how Regina duped so many people in town. He wanted to do follow-up interviews with several people to update his original newspaper stories."

"That means he was going to open old wounds." His mind raced. "What did your dad say about that?"

"He doubted many people would talk to him, but some might have agreed so they could give him a piece of their minds."

"Or beat him within an inch of his life."

"Or give him a bottle of whiskey laced with poison."

Fen dragged a hand across his face. He thought he'd been making progress, but this newest revelation caused him to release a deep sigh.

"You sound discouraged," said Margaret.

"I am. As things stand now, I'll be heading home tomorrow."

Margaret tried to sound upbeat. "You, Bailey, and Lou added more to the case than I thought possible. Dad never gave up and I'm not going to, either."

"I hate to dump the case back in your lap, but I've hit a dead end. Perhaps I can come back after Christmas and pick up where we left off."

"That may not be necessary. Hotel checkout isn't until eleven o'clock tomorrow morning. Plenty of time for a Christmas miracle."

After signing off, Fen went back to work by adding an outline of the bottom lip. He forced himself to focus on the minute details of Regina's lipstick-covered lips. The key features were complete.

He spent another two hours of adding details to eyebrows, nose, eyes, and lips before tossing his pencil into a box. "This is hopeless."

While gathering Bailey's individual sketches of Charley's facial features, he inspected them one last time. She did good work.

He went back to his easel to gather his pencils and inspected the trio of images one last time. "No way!" An explosion of laughter followed. Everything fell into place as if an unseen magnet was fitting metal puzzle pieces together. "Looks like we won't be leaving town tomorrow."

He grabbed his phone, called Lou, and shouted, "Merry Christmas!"

"Thanks," said Lou. "And a very merry Christmas to you."

"It will be if my favorite research assistant will find out a couple of things tonight."

"I'm busy enjoying a crackling fire and hot chocolate."

"You can keep enjoying them. All you need is your computer. If I'm right, it will be a very special Christmas present to Hap."

"You solved the murder?"

"That's not all." He gave her a brief explanation and issued the assignment. He finished with, "Call Bailey. Have her and J.W. come to the hotel tomorrow. I'll reserve a conference room."

Fen's next phone call went to Margaret. He began by saying, "We have our Christmas miracle. Let me explain."

Once he finished, she asked, "Are you sure?"

"I'm positive, but Lou is following up on a couple of things. I'll need you to do whatever it takes to get some people to the hotel conference room tomorrow evening at six." He gave her the list and told her Bailey and J.W. would be there. "It's up to you to make sure Hope is there."

Chapter Twenty-Eight

Fen gave a passing thought to going to the parade but decided against it. The odds of running into Hope were slim, but he didn't want to spoil her day by a chance encounter. Instead, he stayed in his room, gathered reports from Lou and Margaret and allowed things to unfold. He also outlined how he'd conduct the evening's meeting. There were a lot of moving parts, and he expected a fair amount of acrimony.

The knock on his door sounded a little before noon. Fen greeted Bailey and J.W. with, "I wasn't sure what time you'd be here."

J.W. answered, "We waited until the parade started."

Bailey chimed in, "Parades are major headaches for cops. So many streets to block off. I knew the chances of us getting pulled over were next to nothing."

Once again, she'd thought ahead and planned the best possible time to drive through town.

Fen pointed to a chair and love seat. "Are you hungry?"

J.W. held up his hand. "We ate before we left Oklahoma."

"I'm guessing you stayed at one of the casino's hotels. How was it?"

Bailey's face brightened. "It was great. J.W. took his art supplies. We worked a deal to set up our easels and draw caricatures of the guests. We told the manager we'd do it for free, but they comped our rooms, gave us tickets to shows, and allowed us to eat at the buffet."

J.W. gave a word of correction. "*We* didn't work a deal. Bailey did. She knocked out a caricature of a newlywed couple in front of the Christmas tree and showed it to the manager. He put us to work right away, and we have a standing invitation to come back."

A brief silence allowed Bailey to change the subject. "Lou told me you have surprises in store for people this evening."

"Thanks to you. The only wild card is if Margaret can't convince the people I selected to come to our little gathering. It won't change the outcome, but it will be more entertaining if she gets everyone here."

"Don't worry about Mom," said J.W. "I'll call her later and tell her where and when to meet me."

"What will you two do until this evening?" asked Fen.

Bailey smiled. "Do you mind if J.W. uses your bathroom to change into his bathing suit? The last time we tried to go swimming, things didn't work out."

The day passed with reports coming in from Lou and Margaret. Each one confirmed what he thought. Surprises were in store for quite a few people. He went to the conference room thirty minutes ahead of time and set up two easels.

Lou and Hap were the first to arrive. Fen asked, "Any trouble getting through town?"

"We came in Hap's truck," said Lou. "I didn't want to chance coming in my car." She cut her eyes to Hap. "Besides, I have an invitation to spend Christmas with Hap and Margaret."

A slight blush rose into Hap's smiling face. "If this comes together the way I hope it does, she'll need to stick around town and write a bunch of stories."

"That will give Thelma something to complain about, which will take the pressure off me and Bailey."

Carmine Dumbrowski strode into the room with a look of confusion furrowing his brow. "A lady detective called me and told me to report to you. What's going on?"

Fen nodded. "She'll be here in a few minutes. Please have a seat. There're several other people coming. We'll get started as soon as everyone arrives."

Margaret came in next. She held Cleo Clayton's hand and spoke in a soft tone. "There's nothing to worry about. I'll sit you away from everyone, and you don't have to say anything. You'll like what you're going to hear."

The former bank manager looked frail and frightened, with head down and hand trembling. Fen questioned his decision to include her, but believed it was worth it. She needed the healing that truth brings. It was a gamble, but one worth taking.

Mason came next. White tape still held his nose in place. He looked at the assembly with questioning eyes but didn't say anything as he took a seat.

The next to arrive was Hope. She took one look at the room's occupants and raised her chin along with her voice. "Where's my son?"

"He's close," said Fen. "Please come in and have a seat."

"I'll have a dozen cops here in five minutes if you don't produce him now."

"No, you won't," said Margaret. "I've spoken to the chief and explained what's going to happen. He told me to handle this meeting."

"We'll see about that." She reached into her purse and pulled out her phone.

Margaret spoke with conviction. "You're wasting your time. After the parade he left to go deer hunting in the Big Bend."

Hope's eyes flashed with fury. "You'll regret this. You can kiss your job goodbye."

Hap stood. "Hope, you're going to feel a lot better about life when you leave here tonight. Until then, if you don't put a sock in that mouth of yours, you'll have some serious apologizing to do."

"I don't apologize. It's a sign of weakness."

"You're wrong, Mother." The voice came from the doorway. "It's a sign of strength." J.W. and Bailey filed in.

"Where have you been?"

"Having the time of my life."

Hope took long steps toward her son and grabbed him by the hand. "We're leaving, and you're in more trouble than you thought possible."

He jerked away and stood towering over her, speaking loud without words.

"No one's leaving," said Margaret.

Hope spun to face the threat to her authority. "Who's going to stop me?"

"I am." Margaret squared her shoulders. "You threatened a peace officer and I'm detaining you. You have a choice of sitting down with or without handcuffs."

"Sit down and be quiet, Mother."

Stunned into silence and facing the hard gazes of her son and a police detective, Hope sat and seethed.

Fen took over. "This first part shouldn't take long. I'd like to announce that because of the hard work of many people in this room, I'm confident we know who killed Charley Cleg. We also know the location of Regina Cox."

He didn't wait for questions after making the proclamation. "Now that everyone's listening, I'll explain. This was a baffling case because of its scope. So many people fell for the scam perpetrated by Regina. Charley added fuel to the fire by writing a flurry of caustic stories. Did anyone notice how he focused on the local residents and not those from other parts of the state or country?"

"I did," said Hap. "It made no sense to go after the locals."

"That threw me for a loop, too. Why would a local boy go to so much trouble to hurt people from his hometown?"

"He was evil," said Hope.

Fen nodded in agreement. "He was also ambitious. He wanted to make it big in his career and knew he needed stories that would make top newspapers sit up and take notice. Locals were easy pickings because he already knew them, including his own family."

"Amen to that," said Mason. "He brought up some real personal stuff about me and my ex-wife."

"So what?" said Hope. "We all know he focused on locals."

Lou broke in, "That doesn't explain how he knew so much about them, especially the socialites. He came from modest means and never rubbed shoulders with the ladies in the garden club or the church socials. If you go back and read his articles, over half were about women who had money and social standing."

"Like me," came a soft voice from the back of the room.

Fen cast his gaze to the former bank vice president. "Exactly, Cleo. Did you ever meet Charley?"

"Only once. I knew he was a reporter, but I never spoke to him until he questioned me about my role and the bank's involvement. All I ever said was no comment. Yet, he knew so much about me. Personal stuff."

"You've made your point, Mr. Maguire," said Hope. "Where is Regina?"

Fen moved to the two easels he'd set up. He placed the picture he'd drawn of the waterfall, the tiny skyscraper, and the completed sketch of Regina. "Drawing and painting help me think. Most of the time I get answers to tough questions while I'm focused on my work. I had the idea that I could solve these crimes if I lost myself in drawing these two scenes. Bailey was tasked with sketching Charley's facial features, before completing his portrait. She didn't have time to complete that assignment because I needed her to start drawing Regina."

He took a deep breath and pointed to the three-part drawing. "What do the three things on this page have in common?"

J.W. answered. "They portray deception."

"That's right. There was no longer a natural waterfall on the Wichita River, so the town built one. The world's smallest skyscraper lost investors a lot of money back in the day. Both show that things weren't as they appeared. Fast forward a number of years, and Regina came to town. In only a year's time, she worked her way into the fabric of the upper crust of society. Once in, she pulled off a massive fraud."

"We all know that. Where is she?" demanded Hope.

"She's dead," said Fen.

The room stayed silent for a few seconds before Hope challenged him again. "Prove it."

"I'll give you that honor. Come up here."

"I don't know what kind of game this is, but I'm not playing."

Carmine, the maintenance worker, stood. "I'll do it. I may be from out of state, but that woman cheated me out of more than money. I've worked myself to the bone getting out of debt. What do you want me to do?"

Fen motioned for him to come forward. "It's simple,

Carmine. Bailey drew detailed sketches of various parts of Charley's face. Carefully study her drawings of the nose, mouth, eyebrows, and eyes. Don't worry about the ears."

Carmine took his time in studying each drawing. He finished and asked, "Now what?"

"Move over here and study the drawing of Regina's face."

He studied it for at least a minute. The light of revelation came into his eyes. "It can't be."

"But it is," said Fen.

"What are you two babbling about?" demanded Hope.

Carmine turned to face her. "The faces are the same."

"That's impossible."

"Come see for yourself."

Hope took Bailey's individual drawings of Charley's facial features and compared them with Fen's completed drawing of Regina's face.

Unbelief etched Hope's face until Margaret said, "I ran the photos of Charley and Regina through facial recognition. They're the same person. Fen wasn't lying when he said Regina was dead. She, or rather he, is awaiting burial under the name Charley Cleg."

Mason focused his gaze on his brother's portrait. "When Charley was young, he liked to pretend he was someone else and play dress-up like a superhero. I never thought he would pretend to be a woman."

Hope's hands were shaking as she put the sketches back on the easels. "She was so feminine. I had her in my home several times. I confided in her."

"So did I," said Cleo from the back row. "It all makes sense now. I never told Charley about the pressure the bank's board of directors put on me to make loans, but I told Regina. She acted like she really cared, but all the time I was giving Charley a story that would cost me my job and reputation."

Fen looked at Lou. "Help me out."

Lou turned in her chair to face Hope. "In searching newspaper photos, I noticed something—Regina always wore a scarf. I thought it was a marketing ploy, similar to the way some men wear a bow tie. In this case, Charley was covering his Adam's apple. That fact, along with Fen's sketches, confirmed that we had discovered Regina Cox."

Carmine tilted his head. "Where's the money?"

Fen pointed to Margaret. "Your turn."

Margaret shook her head. "You're on a roll. Finish what you started."

He took in a deep breath. "There's still a lot of police work to be done, and it's going to take time. Margaret is seeking help from the Texas Rangers to track down the money. Now that they know Regina was really Charley, they know where to look."

Hope choked out, "Where is it?"

"To answer that," said Fen, "we must first identify who killed Charley."

Chapter Twenty-Nine

Hope's face took on an ashen pallor. Fen moved on without delay, "Solving the murder was the easier part of these two cases. We used standard police procedures."

Carmine was sitting on the edge of his seat. "What did you do? The closest I get to cops is watching television. I'd like to know how you track down a killer."

Fen called Bailey to help him. "Put up a clean piece of paper and draw a circle the size of a salad plate in the center."

She did so as he continued to speak, "Now write *close family* inside the circle. When you finish, draw a bigger circle around the first one and write *friends, distant family, and co-workers* inside that one."

Bailey caught up with him. "What's next?"

"Another circle outside the last one. Write *enemies and people with grudges* in that one."

"Any more?" asked Bailey.

"One more. Write *random* in the last circle."

"Thanks, Bailey. You can sit down."

Fen looked at Margaret. "Show me where Jay Grimes began his investigation into Charley's death."

Margaret came to Bailey's drawing. She pointed at the outer circles. "He wanted it to be Bailey because there was a connecting door between the two rooms. That didn't work out, so he worked his way back toward the center.

"I'm not saying he was wrong to suspect Bailey, but that's not where you'll find most killers. I'll point to where we found the person who killed Charley."

Margaret tapped the innermost circle. "Right here. It was family."

Mason sprang to his feet. "With all I've been through, my name better not come out of your mouth."

Fen patted the air with the palms of his hands. "Sit down, Mason. It's not you or your mother."

Wanting to build his case, Fen raised his voice. "A second thing that's important to remember is that Charley orchestrated a scheme that brought him millions of dollars. Regina ceased to exist after she withdrew the money. Charley believed the police might monitor his expenses because he knew so much about the investors. That left a mystery person, someone Charley trusted with the money."

Hope asked, "Hap, how much did you look into Charley's finances?"

"I checked after he started writing articles, but that was because I'd checked everyone else's and ran out of leads. After all, he hadn't invested anything, and there was no motive. As far as I could tell, he was an energetic reporter looking to make a name for himself."

Fen jumped back in. "The key to stealing that much money is to move it quick and keep moving it. The mistake most thieves make is to spend too much money too fast, but Charley was smart about that. He scored a job with a decent salary, lived modestly in a one-bedroom apartment, and kept to himself. Years passed without him dipping into the big nest egg. The only major purchases he made was a home near Eagle Mountain Lake and a set of very expensive golf clubs."

Hap spoke up. "We didn't know that until Fen gave Lou a street address and told her to find out who owned the property. Charley apparently bought it as an investment and put it into a rental program that he managed."

"This is all very interesting," said Hope. "Are we getting close to the punch line?"

"Relax and enjoy the ride, Mom."

Hope crossed her arms and leaned back, so Fen continued, "Lou went to Fort Worth and spent the day talking to Charley's co-workers. I'll let her tell you what she found out."

"I learned Charley was a loner and a mediocre investigative reporter. The best reporters are tenacious when gathering information. In the years that he was with the Fort Worth newspaper, he never broke a major story. His editor was going to fire him after the holidays."

"Tell them about you going to his apartment," said Fen.

"It wasn't much to talk about, but he had a very expensive set of golf clubs in the closet."

Fen smiled at the group. "Does anyone want to take a stab at who the killer might be?" His gaze shifted around the room. "If you already know, you can't guess."

No hands went up.

"I'll give you some more clues." He moved to the circles that Bailey drew. "I'd count the killer in the inner circle, even though you might move her out to the next one."

No one responded, so he said, "One more clue. She owns a home in a golf course community near Eagle Mountain Lake."

Hope shouted, "It's Lisa Cleg. Charley's ex-wife. She's sort of family, but not really."

Fen affirmed her choice with a minor correction. "You're right, but her legal name is Lisa Stuart. She took her maiden name back when they divorced. The home Charley bought as rental property shares a privacy fence with Lisa's home. There's a gate between the two yards."

"Does she have the money?" asked Hope with a plea in her voice.

Fen looked at Margaret. "From here on, it's Detective Sibley's show. She's been busy."

Margaret took her place at the front of the room. "Fen noticed the gate connecting the two yards and thought it strange. That's what gave him the idea that Lisa was in on the fraud all along. Charley and Lisa spent years planning and implementing their scheme to steal from the people in Wichita County. I also discovered she was still the beneficiary of his life insurance."

She took a step forward. "After Fen explained everything to me last night, I asked Dad for advice. He suggested I call the Texas Rangers. We obtained a warrant and arrested Lisa this morning at her home. We spent the day at the Tarrant County Jail interviewing her. She'll transfer Monday morning to Wichita County where the district attorney will eventually meet with her and her attorney. The Rangers, Dad, and I will add to the evidence as it comes in. They'll probably trade years in jail in exchange for the money she and Charley stole."

"What about the murder charge?" asked Mason.

"We took Lisa's DNA samples. It's likely she packed Charley's suitcase and transferred her DNA when she did. We're waiting on the report from forensics." Margaret summarized. "Fen was right. Look for family first, and follow the money."

Carmine asked, "What's the chance of getting some money back?"

"Good, but it will take time. The D.A. will have fraud and murder charges to bargain with. Lisa's attorney will likely dribble out information on where she has the money stashed. Like I said, money for years behind bars, but we might be able to speed up things by discovering where the money is without her telling us. It will be much easier to find now that we know Lisa has access to it."

Fen stood. "Be sure to read tomorrow's newspaper. Lou has a dynamite front-page story that covers most of what we discussed tonight."

Lou pouted as she said, "I hate it when Fen won't let me tell the complete story."

"What do you mean?" asked Hope.

"He won't let me put any of our names in it. Margaret and Hap get all the credit."

Bailey and J.W. were the first to leave the room. Bailey returned in less than a minute and stood by Fen. Hope joined them and tilted her head. "Where's J.W.?"

Bailey put on her best look of innocence. "He has a date."

Hope's eyelids fluttered. "A date? With who?"

"His girlfriend. She's an international student from Scotland. Beautiful red hair and green eyes to die for. J.W. told me you never allowed him to date a girl more than a few times. We pretended to be an item so he could continue seeing Corine. Don't blow a gasket when he tells you she might be the one for him."

Hope swallowed hard. "It seems I owe both of you an apology."

Fen swiped away the offer. "Have supper with us, and we'll call it even."

Chapter Thirty

The stairway steps creaked as Fen climbed to Bailey's studio apartment. He smiled at the two-foot monogrammed stocking hanging on her door. The house looked more like Sally would have had it this Christmas. She would have liked Bailey.

Fen tapped on the door and waited, but his young protégé didn't answer. Knocking harder, he heard a faint moan. Three more knocks and footsteps sounded. The door flew open and she appeared, digging sleep from her left eye.

"What's wrong?" she asked.

He took a step back. "Nothing's wrong, other than you look like you slept with your head in a pencil sharpener. There's a foot of fresh snow and it's going to melt if we don't hurry. Get dressed if you want to paint a landscape of snow covering the river valley on Christmas day. This may be a once-in a-lifetime chance."

It was as if someone had turned on a light switch. There wasn't much that could get Bailey wide awake before dawn, but the promise of capturing a remarkable scene did it.

"Get me a cup of coffee. I'll grab everything I need and meet you in the den."

"Bundle up. It's cold outside."

Once downstairs, Bailey made a beeline to the back porch. The first rays of a sunburst poked through the quickly scattering clouds. Bailey held her insulated mug in one hand and an easel in the other. Fen followed her with a folding table and her box of pencils.

She whispered, "It's perfect. This landscape will be in oils."

"Take plenty of photos," said Fen. "It's not likely you'll get another chance to get such a perfect sunrise and a pristine blanket of snow."

She retrieved the phone from her pocket and captured the moment.

"Which scene do you like the best?"

Excitement filled her voice. "All of them. I want to paint the entire river valley, but I need to focus on something special. Look! There's steam rising from the river." She pointed. "I'll zoom in and capture the snow in the foreground with the mist over the river as it makes a bend. There's an interesting spot where the trees part and the river curves to the east."

"Good choice. I'm going to focus on the high ground as it drops into the valley."

Thirty minutes later, Fen's fingers were numb. He turned to face Bailey. "Are you ready to go in?"

"No, but my feet are." She scanned the scene one more time. "It's so quiet and beautiful. I've never seen a white Christmas."

"Make sure you take your boots off. Thelma will have a fit if you track snow in."

Closing the door behind them, Fen took in the shining lights of the massive fir decked out with garland and ornaments.

"You and Thelma did a good job with the tree. It looks nice. I think Sally would have approved."

"Thanks, it was fun. You have a lot of decorations to choose from. We didn't do much for Christmas when I was growing up."

Fen swallowed hard. "Yeah, Sally loved Christmas." He turned toward the kitchen. "Let's get some coffee and warm up."

They both grabbed a snowman mug, filled it with coffee and sat at the kitchen table. The sizzle of bacon frying accompanied Thelma's strident voice. "Lou should be parked at that table, too. She's on my naughty list for not comin' home after you solved the case. It makes no sense for her to get involved with a man that lives halfway to Canada."

Fen kept the mug close to his mouth so he could take a sip and avoid contradicting her. Bailey enjoyed their frequent sparring, so she waded into the choppy water. "I think it's cool that Lou's having a Christmas romance. Knowing her, it won't last, but it'll give her a good boost going into the new year. She's also working on follow-up stories."

"Don't that newspaper in Wichita Falls have their own reporters?" asked Thelma.

Bailey grinned. "Of course they do, but they're not as good as Lou. Besides, she's writing the next chapter of her book while she has some time."

Thelma looked up from the skillet and turned to face the table. "What book?"

"Lou's compiling a book of all the cases we work together. By we, I mean Fen, me, and her."

"How many is it now?"

Fen joined the conversation. "Four so far, but I'm sure that will change. Chuck and Candy will be here this afternoon. I'm learning to get nervous when he calls to say he and Candy would like to talk."

Thelma snorted out a loud, "Humph! You got no business travelin' all over the state fixin' problems for people. I say you should stay close to home and live like normal folk."

Fen countered with, "You should be proud of me. I left a lot of the work for the police to do this time." He knew the next statement would get a rise out of Thelma, but he said it anyway. "I could have stayed; Hope asked me to."

"You'd be lookin' for a new cook and housekeeper if you hadn't come home. Your place is here, especially at Christmas. You ought to know better than anyone you'd be miserable if you spent the holidays away from home. You just try bein' gone from Christmas and I'd send Sam to get you, and when you got back, I'd get a switch from a peach tree and—"

Bailey couldn't hold in her laugh, which caused Fen to bust out, too.

"It ain't funny," said Thelma.

"It is, because Hope didn't invite me."

"Still ain't funny."

He could always tell by the way Bailey's eyebrows came together that she had a question. He put down his mug. "Is something bugging you about the case?"

"Yeah. Why did Lisa kill Charley? They pulled off an almost perfect crime. All they had to do was spend the money slowly, and they could have lived happily ever after."

"I wondered the same thing," said Thelma.

"Me, too. That's why I called Margaret for an update. After the district attorney made the plea bargain agreement with Lisa's attorney, Margaret had an off-the-record talk with her. To make a long explanation short, Lisa gradually fell out of love. Another contributing factor was boredom."

Bailey, still wearing her wool cap, shook her head. "You'll need to expand that explanation if you want it to make sense."

Fen placed his palms on the table. "All right, you'll get the longer version, and I know you'll be able to relate to part of it. How did it make you feel when you were stealing cars in Houston?"

"It was a rush, especially if the cops chased us."

"Did you plan it out much?"

"Hardly any thought went into it."

"Now think about how exciting it would be to plan a crime for years. This wouldn't be an ordinary crime. It would involve pulling the wool over the eyes of an entire town, and even the entire country. It was a substantial risk, but think about the rewards. For years, the plan consumed you."

"Keep talkin'," said Thelma.

"A day didn't pass that Lisa didn't experience pressure. Charley could get caught every time he dressed as a woman. He might bring her down with him. There she was, a woman with a clean record going along with the plan of a cross-dressing man to steal money from innocent people."

Fen leaned forward. "And then it was all over. Lisa and the man she still considered her husband had millions of dollars. In a matter of days, she'd shifted the money into so many fake businesses that it would take a small army of accountants to track it down. If there was ever a question about her guilt, it ended when she made the transfers."

"They were home free," said Bailey.

"It depends on how you define freedom." Fen took a sip from his mug. "They were so blinded by money they didn't consider what being separated would do to their relationship. They tried to make it work when they bought Charley a home directly behind Lisa's. But by that time, Lisa was used to the attention from the men at the golf club."

Fen ran a finger around the rim of his mug. "They also tried to make their relationship work by taking trips to play golf, but it was too late."

"Why?" asked Thelma.

"According to Margaret," said Fen, "Lisa told her Charley hated golf. Playing it was a temporary release from guilt for Lisa and torture for Charley. It led to arguments that morphed into mistrust. Lisa thought Charley's idea of going back to Wichita Falls for follow-up research on a book was the most foolish thing he could do. It would only bring attention back to the crime they'd committed. She wanted out of the partnership for good. But how?"

"Poison in a bottle of whiskey," said Thelma.

"Exactly," said Fen. "She knew his favorite brand and wrapped it in fancy paper with a bright red bow. Little did he know it would be the last present he'd ever open."

Thelma wrinkled her brow into a question. "Was it Lisa that burned the popcorn?"

Fen nodded. "She took her own car to Wichita Falls. Charley put a rock in the side door of the hotel to keep it open. Lisa went up the stairway to his room and gave him his Christmas present. While I was sleeping and Bailey and J.W. were swimming, Charley was drinking and dying. It was taking longer than Lisa thought, and Charley wanted a snack."

Bailey finished the story. "She was understandably nervous and put way too much time on the microwave."

Fen finished. "The smoke alarm going off worked in Lisa's favor. She was one of many wearing winter gear with her head and face covered as she went outside."

Thelma said, "I guess the moral of this story is like I always say, 'Don't drink whiskey.'"

Fen and Bailey traded grins. Bailey quickly changed the

subject. "Do you think Chuck and Candy will have another case for us?"

"They'd better not," said Thelma. "You two need to stay home until spring and catch up on your painting."

"Speaking of," said Fen. "Hope commissioned two paintings. One from me and one from Bailey."

"She did?" said Bailey with eyes wide with excitement.

Fen's weak nod communicated it was no big deal. "She wants landscapes of our river valley. That's why I made sure you were up so early. You can do the winter scene and I'll do a summer landscape. Use oils and take your time. You're being well paid for your talent."

Bailey bolted upright in her chair. "Hallelujah! I'm finally graduating from acrylics."

"Consider it a Christmas present."

Bailey rose from her chair, came behind him, and gave him a two-armed hug and a kiss on the cheek. "What a fabulous Christmas present."

His voice cracked when he tried to respond.

Thelma had no trouble with her vocal cords. "You get back in your chair, young lady. I know you. You're goin' to stay holed up in that studio upstairs until we have to pull you out kickin' and screamin'. Three times a day, you need to park yourself at this table. I don't want you gettin' sick again."

Bailey ran to Thelma and gave her a big hug. "You're the best, Thelma, but don't act surprised if I miss a meal. Fen's teaching me how to lose myself in my work."

Bailey took off like a shot. "I'll be back in a flash. Need to check my supplies."

Thelma tented her hands on her hips and turned to Fen. "Aren't you gonna' say something to her?"

"Not a word. It's Christmas day, and it doesn't matter about her supplies. She has a full set of oils and brushes under the tree. She's easy to buy for."

Thelma came and sat in the chair Bailey had vacated. "You know the day will come when she won't be here at Christmas."

Fen's nod took its time going down and back up. "I prefer not to think about that today."

Thelma patted his hand. "Me, neither. I'll take a plate to her. After all, it's Christmas."

Thank you for reading *Murder On The Wichita*. I hope Fen and his team kept you turning the pages to find out whodunit! If you loved it, please consider leaving a review at your favorite retailer, Bookbub or Goodreads. Reviews are the lifeblood of books and *your* review will keep the lifeblood flowing!

If you would like to know when I release the next book in the Fen Maguire Mysteries, join my reader community. You'll be among the first to know about new releases, discounts and recommendations. After you sign up you'll receive the first perk of being a Mystery Insider, the prequel to the Fen Maguire Mystery series!

Happy Reading!

Bruce

Scan above or go to brucehammack.com/the-fen-maguire-mysteries-prequel.

Drawing from his extensive background in criminal justice, Bruce Hammack writes contemporary, clean read detective and crime mysteries. A huge fan of Hercule Poirot and Sherlock Holmes, he believes the world can never have enough whodunits!

He is the author of the Smiley and McBlythe Mysteries, the Fen Maguire Mysteries and the Star of Justice series. Having lived in eighteen cities around the world, he now shares his home in the Texas hill country with his wife of thirty-plus years.

Follow Bruce on Amazon, Bookbub and Goodreads for the latest new release info and recommendations. Learn more at brucehammack.com.

www.ingramcontent.com/pod-product-compliance
Lightning Source LLC
Chambersburg PA
CBHW061817190726
48289CB00007B/2227